The Surgeon's Blade

By Faith Mortimer

Also by Faith Mortimer:

"The Crossing" – *A Voyage of High Adventure, Action and Romance across Two Generations*

"The Assassins' Village" – *A Classic Murder Mystery in a Cyprus Village (featuring* **Diana Rivers** *Novelist & Amateur Sleuth)*

"Children of the Plantation" – *A* **Diana Rivers** *Mystery set in Malaysia*

"The Bamboo Mirror" – *An Anthology of Short Mysteries – introducing Diana Rivers*

(all available as a paperback or eBook)

About the author.

Faith Mortimer was born in Manchester and educated in Malaya, Singapore and Hampshire. After training to become a nurse she switched careers and ran various travel and sport-related companies. On completion of her Yachtmaster examinations and after studying for a Science degree, she and her husband Chris, sailed their yacht across the Atlantic and enjoyed many years exploring the seas. It was during this time whilst living on board, that Faith wrote her first book; *'The Crossing'.* Now back on terra firma, they divide their time living in the United Kingdom and Cyprus. *'The Assassins' Village',* Faith's second novel, which introduced writer and amateur sleuth *Diana Rivers,* was published in 2011, closely followed by her third, **'C***hildren of the Plantation'.* An Anthology of Short Mysteries, *"The Bamboo Mirror"* was published in 2011.

You can get in touch with Faith via her website, Facebook, and Twitter.

www.faithmortimerauthor.com
www.facebook.com/FaithMortimer.Author
http://twitter.com/FaithMortimer

The Surgeon's Blade

Copyright © Faith Mortimer 2012

A CIP catalogue record of the title is

available from the British Library.

ISBN: 978-0-9569318-3-2

First Published in 2012

Published by
Topsails Charter
Southampton

Acknowledgements

A. Big Thank You to my editor Catherine and to my husband Chris for their invaluable assistance and patient support

The Surgeon's Blade

Prologue

Playing this game was a major enjoyment. It had been played many times before, and this time, it was proving even more of a thrill.

The watcher spotted her immediately. She was seated at a table for two, and from the number of times she had glanced at her watch, it was obvious she had been stood up by her date. The watcher was cautious by nature and covertly observed the woman from a chosen seat which was half-hidden in the shadows behind a potted palm. She was one of those women in their thirties who looked attractive in a quiet, unassuming way and could have been stunning if she had spent more time over her hairstyle and make-up. Her dress was an off-the-rail model, most probably from one of the departmental stores and in a different colour would have enhanced her appeal. Unfortunately, the dull fabric did nothing for her hair and skin colouring.

The watcher had seen her many times around the hospital and knew who she was. She came across as confident and sure of herself as far as her work was concerned.

She now sat alone and forlorn, casting wistful glances at those couples who sat with bent heads sharing a whisper and promise of the night to come. Minutes later, she answered a call on her mobile phone with nervous girlish pleasure, but her face paled in distress as she replaced it into her evening bag. The watcher knew instantly how easy it was going to be and smiling coldly, raised a glass with a slight movement in her direction and offered a silent toast.

Why waste time yearning over a date that would never show when your prayers have been answered, dearest girl, the watcher demanded silently. From now on, you're mine, all mine.

Chapter 1

Three o'clock. The dead hour. It was the rain lashing against the window that woke Libby. Cursing under her breath, she glanced at her clock on the bedside cabinet and contemplated the day ahead: nearly three-thirty. She must be mad! At the end of June, the weather really should be fine. 'Flaming June', they called it. Well, there hadn't been too much flaming lately. This was the fourth day in a row of seemingly endless downpours. Dratted weather! Well, she was committed to today's race, and there was nothing she could do but put on a smiling face.

Less than an hour later, showered and dressed, Libby had a quick breakfast of toast and tea and headed for the door. Her cat followed her and meowed loudly as Libby put on her jacket. The fluffy pale ginger cat was obviously thinking her mistress was quite mad, not only for disturbing her slumber at this untimely hour, but for leaving the flat on such a cold and wet day. She sat on the rug looking quite put out.

"Okay, Rommie, I'll see you tonight. Don't fret. The automatic feeder is primed to open for your tea, and I've left you plenty of biscuits in the meantime. If you feel you can bring yourself to use the cat flap, please do, because I don't want any little accidents before I return."

Libby reached down and gave Rommie a final stroke, thinking the cat had the right idea. The morning so far looked awful. She had a quick look round her flat, mentally going through what she would need for the day: wet weather gear, life jacket, and sailing gloves. She noticed the framed degree certificate upon the living room wall. *'Olivia Hunter, registered nurse.'* It was a long time since she'd been called Olivia; not since her parents had been killed. With a shrug, she picked up her bag and locked the door behind her.

Despite the foul weather, she was excited. Being chosen as part of the crew on a fast yacht for the Isle of Wight's prestigious 'Round the Island Race' had a certain cachet, and she had been delighted when Nigel had chosen her. It was Libby's first major sailing event, and Nigel's reputation as a first-class skipper was well known in the yachting fraternity.

Libby unlocked the door to her Mini and threw her bag down onto the passenger seat as the rain splattered against the hood of her jacket. She had promised to pick up Jem, another crew member, before going to the marina where *'Tourbillon'* was moored. Jem, like her, was in his late thirties and worked in the Southampton General Hospital and loved sailing.

Jem was a good friend to Libby and had been instrumental in helping her get the post of junior sister on the general surgery ward. He had been there ever since he had first qualified, whereas Libby had come down from London, looking for a place nearer the sea to work. She had met him on a course in London some years back, and on their first introduction, they had hit it off. Over the past few years, six-foot-four Jem, muscle-bound and fun-loving, had become her biggest friend and confidant.

Libby parked her mini outside the house Jem shared with his partner, and not wishing to antagonise the neighbours by hooting at an early hour, she ran the short distance up the flooded garden path to his door. The door opened at Libby's knock, and Jem ushered her inside.

"I'll be ready in a jiffy. I've just been listening to the national news on the telly. Hang on, I'll turn it off." Jem walked into the living room and crossed over to the television. "It sounds like there really is a dangerous weirdo stalking nurses in London. Another nurse was assaulted during the night at St Thomas's Hospital. Very few details have been released by the police though: only that she's being treated for shock." Shrugging on his waterproof jacket, he picked up a bag lying near the door and gestured to Libby to precede him.

She paused in the doorway. "That's awful. Isn't that the third one now?"

He nodded. "Fourth, if you include that girl who was raped after accepting a drink from a stranger in that Southwark pub. What was it called? I think it was the

Golden Ram or something like that. Of course as that was a sexual attack it might have come from an entirely different person. But all these assaults are now really serious."

"They're awful. I'd forgotten that girl. She wasn't a nurse though, was she?"

"No, but she's a radiographer from the same hospital. The police haven't said for certain whether they think it's the same attacker. And if you add these girls to the two who went missing in the last year or so, then London has a big problem on its hands. Come on, we'd better run for it."

Libby led the way as she pelted back down the path, aiming her remote ignition key at her Mini with Jem close on her heels.

"Blimey! What a day," he said, squeezing his long legs into her car. "Makes you wonder if it'll be worth it."

"It'll be worth it just to see the look on Sebastian Carr's face when we overtake him at the Needles."

Jem gave a chortle of laughter. "You really don't like him, do you?"

"No. He's too self-centred and full of it for my liking."

"And what about our mysterious skipper, Nigel, then? He's from the same mould, same university and medical school. I noticed he's been paying you lots of furtive attention lately when he thinks no one's watching."

Something in his dry tone of voice caused Libby to take her attention off the road to look at him. She knew she had given herself away when she felt her cheeks flame.

"I am right, am I not?" he said gently, giving her a little pat on the knee.

"Yes." She sighed. Jem always guessed when she was seeing someone new, and she had hoped to keep Nigel secret for a tad longer. Nigel had been quite adamant over that. How on earth did Jem do it?

"So what's he like? I know most people think he's the proverbial enigmatic, tall, dark-haired, and good-looking male with wads of cash, but what's he really like under all that expensive designer gear? I bet he's married."

Libby gave a smile, as she remembered the times they had been together recently. Nigel had been very attentive. She thought work and pleasure rarely mixed and despite her best intentions not to get too involved, she eventually succumbed to going out with him.

"He's nice. I know he's a brilliant gynaecological surgeon and apparently can be a bit overbearing in theatre. But outside work he has a good sense of humour, and he treats me well."

"Aha. And?"

"And nothing. Stop it, Jem. That's all you're getting out of me." She swerved to avoid a cyclist wobbling dangerously in the nearside gutter. "We've been out together a few times during the last month, that's all, and for God's sake please don't tell anyone."

"Why ever not? Is Mr St John married then? He's a bit of a dark horse, if you ask me, I'm not sure I trust him."

"No one is asking you to, Jem. But as you asked, and I know you'll never give me any peace, I'll tell you. He was married and is now separated. He and his wife live apart. And as for keeping it quiet, just honour his request, okay?"

There was a short silence as Jem digested this titbit of news, giving her the briefest of nods. "I was right then." He eventually spoke.

"Right about what?"

'Him being married. They're all the same, these big-shot surgeons. He's been here…what, less than a year, and all the single female staff are dying to get their hands on him and about half the married ones too. I wonder what attracts them. He's certainly not my type."

She gave a laugh. "Jem, he's a nice man. Underneath his obvious good connections and money, he wants a normal life just like you and me."

Jem gave her a hurt look as if to say, "Are you being funny?" and turned on the radio. They listened in silence as the newscaster finished his report and changed topics to the weather.

"Well, that sounds a bit more hopeful. *Becoming sunny and drier before mid-morning, with fresh south-westerly winds up to 20 knots*'. We should have a cracking sail once we get out south of the island." He rubbed his hands with glee. "Can't wait."

Libby returned his smile, glad to be off the topic of Nigel. She knew Jem would try keeping her secret safe, but at the same time, she realised he was only human and could easily forget. Juicy gossip sped like wildfire around the hospital, and *she* didn't want to be the subject.

He was right though. Nigel was everything he had said and more. Libby knew about his marriage to Stella. He had been quite open during their second date together, telling her they had married when they were still at medical school and how they had been far too young.

~~~~~

"We should have listened to our parents," he had said. "They urged us to wait until we'd qualified, but like most students we knew best. After we left med school and channelled our time and attention into our chosen career paths, we found we had no time left for each other. Of course, we still had the common ground of medicine to share, but apart from that, there was nothing else. We'd grown up and grown apart from each other. I'm surprised we stayed together as long as we did. It was most probably a mix of things: money, not upsetting our families, apathy, and I suppose convenience. It is often easier to do nothing.

We're still on remarkably good terms and see each other whenever she comes over from the States."

Libby nodded, playing with the stem of her wine glass as he explained. If anything, she was a bit surprised at his openness.

"Were there…did you have any children together?"

"Thankfully, no. Children would have made everything much more complicated. Stella wasn't keen once we'd passed our final exams. She was eager to make her name as a psychiatrist, and she's doing just that in New York and London. Children were way down the list," he said, giving her a grin which made him look younger, boyish even. "No ties there either."

Libby smiled. "She's very clever and a wonderful speaker. I attended a few of her lectures when I was working in London. She certainly knows how to hold an audience, and her voice is captivating with an almost hypnotic effect on the listener."

Pushing back his shirtsleeve, Nigel glanced at his watch, and Libby caught sight of a tattoo on his wrist. She recognised it as Caduceus, the medical symbol or the Physician's Staff tattoo. Nigel caught her look and smiled. "I know. I abhor tattoos too, but Stella made me have it done while we were still students. It was bloody painful too. Do you know the Caduceus derives from the Greek 'karykeion', meaning 'staff of the herald'? It was the symbol of the power to harm or to heal. It appears in images of the ancient Egyptian god of wisdom, Thoth, as a magic rod with twin snakes. I've seen other variations showing a staff entwined with twin serpents, topped with a pair of wings or a winged sun and no snakes. Originally, those twin snakes may have been ribbons attached to the wings, eventually evolving into serpents. Interesting, eh?"

"I know what it represents, but not the full explanation."

"Have you finished? Would you like to come back to my place for a nightcap?"

Libby weighed the pros and cons of spending more time in his company. It was a tempting thought to go and see where he lived and how he spent his free time. It *was* only their second date, and she *did* have to work tomorrow. Spending time back at his place could well lead to things being misunderstood or getting out of control, and that was the last thing she wanted. She considered herself fairly broad-minded. She wasn't a prude but neither was she 'easy'.

She shook her head and gave him a smile, replying. "No thanks. Not tonight, if you don't mind. I have an early start tomorrow. Lisa, Sister Williams, is off, and I'm in charge. We have a full theatre list, so it's bound to be frantic."

Nigel gave her a rueful look as he handed the waiter his credit card. "We'll make it next time then. My apartment has a splendid view of Southampton Water. It looks very romantic lit up at night."

Nigel drove her home and didn't put pressure on her to let him in. He escorted her to her door and, after a chaste kiss, asked to see her again over the weekend. He suggested going for a sail on his yacht, just the two of them, and thrilled with the idea of being on a sailing boat once more, Libby happily agreed.

Libby smiled as she remembered that day. There had been little wind for any real sailing, and they ended up anchoring in a tranquil inlet bay, north of the Isle of Wight. It was far too cold for a swim, but they were content to laze around in the sun, sampling a delicious lunch hamper Nigel had picked up from a ship's caterers before leaving the marina.

It wasn't before long Libby had nodded off, lying on the thick cockpit cushions. Nigel had roused her and suggested a siesta down below. Feeling lethargic and sleepy after a fine lunch and a bottle and a half of champagne, Libby nearly agreed. The main cabin on the Swan was huge, and Libby had done a double take when she had first seen the size of the wide bed. Nigel was considerate and tender, but something made Libby waver. She asked herself, why not? It had been a long time since she had had a proper sexual relationship, and Jem was always telling her she was too picky, too choosy. 'It's about time you lived a little,' Jem had said on more than one occasion. "And I know you won't thank me for this, but it's also time you got over your last disastrous affair."

Libby knew Jem was right, but still she hesitated and put Nigel off with a laugh and a joke. She wanted to be quite sure this time. She had come out of a relationship feeling bruised and hurt far too many times. It wasn't that she didn't enjoy sex – she did, but all too often, she had gone out with men who wanted sex on their first date, and it was becoming tiresome. Libby did have some moral standards.

Libby's introduction to Nigel's yacht had taken place a month ago, and now they were seeing each other on a regular basis a couple of times a week. As far as Nigel was concerned – and he had told her on several occasions – he was serious. Libby kept quiet, feeling there was no rush. She wanted to be sure.

They were discreet in their dating – at Nigel's insistence, as he loathed hospital gossip of any kind – and Libby agreed to go along with his wishes. A secret liaison held a certain sparkle, and Libby found herself caught up in the excitement of it all. They would make their relationship known when they were both ready.

~~~~~

That morning, when they arrived at the marina on the River Hamble, everything was hustle and bustle. Up and down the pontoons, scores of boat crews were checking sails, removing surplus weighty items and generally enjoying the mounting excitement before a big race. The rain had eased off, and a thin, watery sun was peeking between the thinning early-morning clouds.

Libby and Jem picked up their kit bags and made their way down to *Tourbillon's* berth. The Swan 60 was a new design, sixty feet long with a large and well-protected cockpit. Her sea trials had shown superb race performance levels, and she was both comfortable and fast for cruising and offshore racing. Nigel had spared no expense when he purchased this sleek, sexy racing machine.

Tourbillon lay snugly against her fendered berth. Her hull was a gleaming navy blue, polished only days before by the yacht service agents. Her mast stood tall and proud, towering above most of the other craft lying in their own berths. Her halliards were cleated off, and there was only the bare whisper of a ringing as metal struck metal. She looked fantastic, expensive and racy.

As Libby and Jem approached the boat, they espied a tanned Nigel standing on her deck, deep in discussion with another man dressed in white polo shirt and shorts. A blue emblem on his breast pocket portrayed the name of the yacht, and Jem gave Libby a nudge.

"By the look of things, I reckon he'll be the navigator, don't you?"

She didn't have a chance to reply, as Nigel turned towards them at the sound of their footsteps on the wooden pontoon and raised a hand in greeting. When he caught sight of Libby, his smile broadened into one of admiration.

Libby returned his smile, relieved that despite her early start, she had spent some time over her appearance. Nigel was appreciative of her looks, and Libby knew by his high standards, he expected her to look gorgeous at any time, day or night. She sported a new haircut: mid-blonde, short and feathered at the ends. The hairstyle had cost her a lot more than usual, but she knew it suited her elfin face and emphasised her enormous brown eyes. After applying a little discreet lip gloss and a hint of eye shadow, she felt good and knew that Nigel welcomed her effort. He gave her a helping hand as she said with a laugh, "Permission to come aboard, Skip?"

"Libby, you look positively ravishing this morning. I love the new haircut by the way. Morning, Jem. Feeling fit? Hope you're ready to grind those winches!"

"Thank you. Where shall we stow our stuff?" she asked.

"Anywhere below in one of the forward cabins will do. Grab yourself a coffee while you're down there, I'm just going through racing tactics with Ian here. Do you know each other?"

Neither Jem nor Libby had seen him before and shook their heads before they said 'hello'.

Ian was as stocky as Nigel was tall. He had a shock of startling red hair and a mass of freckles covering his pale face. He looked Libby over appreciatively when she turned to leave them and make her way below. He twisted back round to Nigel with a grin. "She's a bit of a looker, isn't she?"

~~~~~

Tourbillon slipped her berth in good time before the race start. Once they had cleared the Hamble River, passing the moored boats along the riverside, they headed south-west down Southampton water and into the clearer waters beyond. The Swan had a deep keel, perfect for slicing through the water, but it meant that careful pilotage had to be maintained through the narrow channels of drifting shingle and sandbanks.

That day's race was the biggest of its kind. Over 16,000 professional and amateur sailors were involved, with 1900 boat entries all vying for glory in their class. The race commenced at Cowes on the Isle of Wight and headed westwards through the challenging Needles channel, south towards St. Catherine's Point, and then back round to the finish line off the Royal Yacht Squadron yacht club in Cowes. The course was 63.3 miles long, and the monohull record stood at 3 hours, 53 minutes and 5 seconds. Nigel's boat was entered along with 23 other boats of the same class, and he was very keen to do well.

Coffee and sandwiches were distributed among the boat crew as they idled to and fro off the Cowes waterfront. Literally hundreds of other craft had turned up to see the start of the race: family yachts, motor boats, ferries, and even a pleasure steamer or two.

Ten minutes before countdown, Nigel, at the helm, was frantic as he jostled for space between two other yachts in his class. The tension was palpable as the countdown begun. The warning guns were fired – three minutes, one minute…they were off!

The open-flat racing boats and the multi-hulls shot ahead, desperate to find clear water and get out of trouble. Libby heard shouting over on her left as she sat with her legs over the starboard side of the yacht. Turning to see what the noise was about, she was in time to see three boats collide with sickening force. She was horrified to see what looked like a brand spanking new yacht with a hole torn in its left side as another one thrashed around with half of its boom and rigging hanging in the sea. She shuddered, unable to believe what had just happened. That could so easily have been them if Nigel wasn't such a good helmsman.

Tourbillon tore along on a close-hauled starboard tack. Her sails filled, and she heeled over in the fresh wind, gaining speed as the crew settled down.

~~~~~

The race was on. *Tourbillon* had found a nice open stretch of water with Nigel's friend and rival, Sebastian, about a quarter of a mile ahead off to their port side. They had rounded the north-west corner of the island without mishap, and the Needles were just ahead. Libby knew all about the Needles: a row of three distinctive stacks of chalk rising out of the sea. There was a buoy that marked 'safe' water, and

Libby knew they had to keep this to port unless they wanted to run aground on the treacherous shingle bank. Many a ship had come to grief there.

Sebastian's own Swan, '*Four Fine Winds*' was maintaining her speed and as Nigel urged his crew to tweak the sails, Libby felt the boat's speed go up a notch as *Tourbillon* settled into her racing groove. Light spray caught Libby in the face, and she laughed in delight as the excitement of the race took hold of her. The yacht came off a wave and surged through the surf.

Four Fine Winds would surely reach the Needles buoy and round it before *Tourbillon*, but Nigel was winding the boat up and putting on the pressure. Hearing Libby's laugh, Nigel gave her a roguish grin and beckoned her over to stand near him.

"Morning, sweetie. Sorry I haven't been able to talk to you yet. How are you doing?" he said, giving her a quick hug with one arm and snatching a surreptitious kiss.

"I'm fine, thanks. This is such fun and so exciting, I can't remember the last time I was part of a race," she said with a laugh. "I'm pleased to be here."

"I'm glad I suggested it. Listen, we'll make tonight special. I've got a huge surprise for you. Now, if only we can beat that bastard to the mark. Can you see him ahead? Where is he exactly?"

Libby moved over to the port side of the yacht to take a peek under the headsail. She knew there were only 100 metres to go before the buoy. Before she could get into position, there was a faint shout coming from their left. Libby heard the indistinct voice across the sea, and suddenly, she realised that someone was yelling, "Water! Water!" The other yacht wanted *Tourbillon* to give way to them.

Four Fine Winds was bearing down on them at an alarming rate. In panic, Libby stood back up to attract Nigel's attention and warn him of the sudden danger. His face was a picture of concentration and determination as he bawled at his crew, "Make ready the chute!" Three hefty crew were dragging the lightweight spinnaker along the deck, getting ready to hoist the sail as soon as they turned the corner. Libby scrambled to the other side of the deck as the wind freshened, and the boat heeled further over, the crew along the side sitting high above the water. She crabbed back to her original position practically on all fours while screaming a warning to Nigel as the shout came again.

This time there was no mistake. "Water!" and Nigel heard the terror in the voice. With a horrified look, he spun the wheel and the massive boom shot over to the other side of the boat.

There was a sickening crunch of metal upon flesh and the boat slewed over. Nigel was bellowing for assistance, the sails were flogging, and Libby was thrown into the water.

"Man overboard!" shouted Jem, rushing to the side and pointing at his stricken friend. Without waiting for an order, he grabbed a lifebuoy and jumped overboard to help her.

~~~~~

Nigel gave the command to slow the boat right down and turn into the wind. The crew released the sheets (ropes) allowing some wind to escape from the sails. A small group gathered on the side of the yacht, looking anxiously down into the turbulent sea, pointing to an unconscious Libby, supported by her lifejacket which had self-inflated. They could see Jem's head and shoulders with the lifebuoy as he battled the short distance against the waves to where she lay, not moving.

As he reached her, a jubilant cry went up, and they shouted encouragement as Jem got the lifebuoy under her arms and manhandled her back towards where *Tourbillon* wallowed in the peaks and troughs of the swell, barely making way.

Four Fair Winds was off to one side and Nigel and Sebastian were having a shouting match. While they were arguing about whose fault the near collision had been, Jem had managed to bring an unconscious Libby alongside, and with help from the other crew, they dragged her on board using a 'man overboard' sling.

Nigel was still at the helm, patently not trusting any of the crew to take over. He had his work cut out to avoid another collision as other yachts streamed past them. Ian came up from below and took in the scene.

"I've radioed a medical pan-pan,' he said, looking grimly at Libby where she lay on the deck, water streaming from her. "They'll be here in a few minutes."

"Good, then we can get underway. Come and take the wheel will you? And for God's sake, watch out. We don't want another mishap. "

Nigel handed the helm over to Ian and climbed out of the cockpit to take a look at Libby. She had a large gash down the right side of her head and was bleeding, her blood mingling with the seawater onto the teak deck.

"Hand me the first aid box. Now let's get her fixed up and ready for the helicopter. It'll be arriving any minute now. Once she's airborne, we can continue with the race. We're nicely ahead of the pack, and I believe we can still pull this off. It was that bugger Sebastian's fault colliding with us, and I'm going to make sure the race marshals know that. Jem, get changed out of those wet clothes. I want you back on the winch as soon as possible!"

Chapter 2

Shocked, Jem looked at Nigel, scarcely believing his ears. What was it he had just said? Irrespective of whose fault it was, Nigel had an unconscious woman, a crew member, lying on his boat. At the very least, he was responsible for the well-being of his crew. Here he was, still anxious to get back into the race. What an unfeeling bastard!

Jem opened his mouth to protest as the first sounds of the helicopter filled the air. He gave a withering look at the top of Nigel's head as he stood up and contemplated what to do.

He was furious with Nigel over his cavalier attitude. "Are you escorting her back to land?" he asked.

Nigel glanced up, a surprised look on his face. "Who me?"

"Yes, you. As the skipper responsible for our well-being and—" He stopped, knowing full well Libby would be upset if she knew he had mentioned her and Nigel's relationship.

"I may be responsible for my crew, but it wasn't my fault. No, I won't be escorting her. The pilot and winch man will have their work cut out without having to worry about another passenger."

"Passenger? She's your bloody girlfriend, isn't she?" Jem growled at him.

Nigel took a quick look round, as if making sure no one else had heard him. The deafening sound from the helicopter drowned out their conversation. "Just keep your thoughts to yourself, matey. Our relationship is purely platonic, and our business is no one else's."

"But surely, you'll want to—"

Nigel stood up as Ian shouted, "The helicopter pilot is on the radio, Skip. They want to talk to you." He tossed a handheld VHF radio over to Nigel once he had re-entered the cockpit and taken back the helm. Ian moved over to Jem, who had remained by Libby's prone body. "How's she doing?"

"Not so good. She's still unconscious and bleeding quite a lot from her wound. It's a horrible gash, and so far, I can't get it to stop bleeding. She might be left with a scar. Pass me another pack of swabs will you?" Feverishly, he tore apart the wrapping and applied a fresh gauze pad to Libby's wound.

'Shame, such a good-looking girl, too. But you never know, they can do wonders these days."

Jem did know because he worked in Accident and Emergency at Southampton General. He was sure, once she received full medical treatment in hospital, her bleeding would cease. At the moment, he was more worried about her mental state. Libby had suffered a considerable blow to her head from the boom as it swung from one side of the boat to the other in the forced gybe. If only that idiot Nigel had been paying more attention. All this could have been avoided. Jem couldn't really understand Nigel's apparent lack of concern. He was after all a man of medicine, a healer, and yet, the race appeared to be uppermost in his mind. Withholding a snort of disgust, Jem decided it took all sorts to make a world. He only hoped Libby knew what she was doing this time. Since he had known her, she had suffered at least two disastrous relationships, and after the last one, her confidence had suffered.

"Right, clear the deck you lot. The winch man is going to pass down a stretcher before the diver comes down. On no account is anyone to touch the hi-line transfer cable until it touches the deck. Do you understand? There can be a hell of a lot of static electricity, and it could kill you. Once it's firmly on the deck, do not tie it on to anything, either. I'm sure you know the drill." Nigel bellowed. "Once she's aboard, we'll get going again."

There was a series of surprised mutterings at this, and Jem was gratified to see quite a few of the crew looked askance at their skipper. Privately, he considered Nigel to be an unfeeling bastard.

"Come on, look lively. Get the sails ready! We've got a race. We're not finished yet. We can still do this."

Jem could have hit him.

Chapter 3

Libby felt strange. She was nursing an almighty headache and there was a loud ringing in her ears. Never had she felt so incapacitated. She knew that if she sat up she would be violently sick. Her whole body felt as if it was vibrating, and there was a deafening rumble around her. She gave a groan and closed her eyes.

"Take it easy love. Just lie still." A dismembered voice muttered in her ear, and opening her eyes, a face swam into her vision. It was slightly skew-whiff and blurred, but squinting, she could definitely see a face.

"Can you hear me?" he asked, bending down towards her ear. She nodded and wished she hadn't, as everything went black, and a whooshing noise replaced the drone. "You've had an accident. Do you remember?"

She struggled to frame the word 'no'.

"Don't try to move or talk until I've done some obs. You've got a nasty wound on your forehead, which I'm going to dress. This might hurt a bit. It's only a medicated swab, nothing more."

Libby winced as she felt a cold, wet compress upon her face. The astringent antiseptic bit into her raw lesion. "Ow!" she moaned, opening her eyes wide with surprise.

"There. Nearly all done. What's your name? Can you tell me?"

Libby thought. Nothing. The more she thought, the more she panicked. *What was her name?* She gave a slight shake of her head and realised tears were welling up. What had happened? Why was she so wet?

"I can't remember," she whispered. "What happened? Why am I so wet and—" She struggled to sit up. "Where am I?"

The uniformed man placed a hand on her shoulder, gently pushing her back down. "I'm Jack, by the way. You've been in a sailing accident. Do you remember that?"

"No!" Waves of nausea rushed over her. She lay back, beginning to shake with shock.

"Okay, just take it easy. I'll explain. You were taking part in a sailing race. I believe there was a collision between the yacht you were on and another. During the collision you went overboard. That's why you are so wet. You're now on the Solent Rescue helicopter, *India Juliet*, and we're flying you to Southampton Hospital."

For some reason, the hospital meant something to Libby, but she couldn't remember what. She struggled with the grey woolliness in her brain. "Why can't I remember?"

"By the look of your injury, I would say you hit your head before you went overboard. It's probably only temporary, and things will begin to come back after you've rested. You've got quite a bump there. I can tell you that your name is Libby. Your boat skipper gave that to us."

Libby? Libby? Still nothing. She lay still as misery flooded through her. What on earth was going to happen to her?

"We'll be there in a short while. Now, if I can just take your blood pressure."

Libby felt a cuff tighten around her arm. She strained to look around her without moving her position, and as her vision cleared, realised she could see the pilot. She could hear him as he talked into his helmet mike. At that moment, he glanced in the rear mirror in front of him and met her eyes. Despite herself, Libby felt a frisson of interest. She saw nice eyes, a deep green and unusual shade of hazel, green and blue with brown flecks. As she watched him, he swivelled round in his seat with a shaken look. After a moment, his face cleared and he gave her a smile. There was something about that smile that made her feel secure. Perhaps she was worrying unnecessarily, and everything was going to be all right.

The pilot turned back to his controls, and Jack said they were about to land. The new helipad at the hospital was in sight.

~~~~~

Libby was dozing when she realised there was someone in the room with her. As she opened her eyes, she noticed the soft evening sunshine throwing shadows on the walls, and with a start, she turned to find the chair next to her bed occupied. He was dark-haired with conventional good looks, a tanned face, blue eyes, and a long aquiline nose. He was dressed in sailing clothes: a polo shirt, trousers and deckshoes.

"Libby, darling. I'm sorry if I woke you, but the staff said you were awake. I've only just managed to get here to see you. The traffic from the Hamble was horrendous."

Libby stared blankly at the face before her. She had no idea who he was.

"I'm sorry," she began. "But...who are you?" Her voice wavered.

"Darling, don't you remember? It's me, Nigel."

She hesitated, then, "No. I don't know you. I can't even remember who I am." To her horror, tears were gathering and threatening to roll down her face. "How did you manage to get in? I told the staff I didn't want visitors!"

"Darling, hush. It's all right. Why wouldn't they let me in, they could hardly refuse could they? I am one of the senior medical staff here. Of course, they don't know about our personal relationship."

"Relationship?" Libby frowned.

"Yes. Don't tell me you've forgotten we're engaged?"

Engaged? Horrified, Libby struggled to clear her head. Apparently she was engaged to this man, this stranger, Nigel. She lifted her left hand but her ring finger was bare.

Nigel saw her puzzled look and curled his fingers round her own. "Your ring is at the jewellers, darling. Don't you remember? Since you lost all that weight, your fingers are much more slender. Your ring kept slipping off, and you were afraid of losing it. It'll be ready for you in a day or so." He kissed the tips of her fingers. "Don't worry about anything. You just need to get better."

She choked back a sob. "How can I not worry? I can't remember anything much before I woke up in the helicopter," she said snatching her hand from his – it didn't feel *right* somehow.

"I'm sure your doctor has explained your amnesia to you. You fell overboard and most probably hit your head on the boat's hull. I'm sure your memory will recover in a short time."

"You think so?"

"Of course I do. You have what is known as post-traumatic amnesia. This is a state of confusion that occurs immediately following a violent head injury. You'll probably feel disoriented and unable to remember events that happened before the injury. Sometimes new events can't be remembered either, but it'll resolve itself."

Libby wished she felt reassured, but Nigel's words failed to comfort her.

"I think I can remember a few random things. I don't remember being on a boat. But I do remember driving my car. A Mini, I think it was. Why can I only remember bits and pieces?" she whispered.

"Well, I'm not a neurosurgeon, but I had a word with the doctor on duty before I called in here. He said that about a third of patients with mild head injuries have 'islands of memory' in which the patient can recall only some events. Your consciousness is 'clouded' and you're suffering from retrograde amnesia."

"Yes, he explained that to me too. It's awful only remembering snippets."

"Can you remember where you live?"

She wrinkled her nose as she concentrated hard. "Do I have a flat? I think I'm getting glimpses of something like that."

"Yes, you do. But listen, darling, you were about to leave your flat and move in with me. We had it all sorted out. We decided to live together, don't you remember?"

Libby was shocked and shrank back upon her pillows. "No. I...I don't."

"Well, I can't see that anything's changed. It will be for the best. I can keep a proper eye on you. Darling Libby, you need someone to cherish you."

As Nigel said these words, Libby felt as if she was drowning. Panic gripped her, and an icy feeling ran down her back. It just didn't feel right.

Chapter 4

Libby was woken the next morning by the duty nurse bringing her an early morning cup of tea. The staff nurse bustled around the room, twitching back the curtains and folding a loose over-blanket that had slipped from Libby's bed during her restless night.

"Good morning, and did we sleep well?" she asked with a cheery smile upon her face. She looked older than Libby, short in stature and sported a tanned, plump body.

"Not really," Libby replied. "My headache kept coming and going, despite the painkillers you gave me."

The nurse stopped what she was doing and gave Libby with a sympathetic look.

"Why didn't you ring for some more? You know the drill, being a ward sister yourself. Nobody has to suffer in pain."

Libby looked away from her. Never had she felt so depressed in all her life. To her humiliation, tears began to form. She brushed her eyes with the back of her hand.

"Hey! Don't cry. The doctors think you'll get your memory back. Sometimes it just takes a day or so."

"I know. I'm sorry, it's just that I'm so confused. I don't know who I am or what's going to happen to me. I know I'm Libby and that I work on the general surgical ward, but apart from that, I've only got some snatched glimpses of my past life. You can't know how horrible or frightening it is."

The nurse patted her arm. "Look, just try and relax. I know you think that's impossible, but rest is a good cure. At least you can remember things from yesterday. Imagine if you couldn't retain new knowledge. We've had quite a few amnesiacs in here, and as far as I can remember, all of them got back to nearly normal in time. Some people of course take a few days more than others."

Libby sighed. "What's going to happen to me? When can I go home?"

"I'm not sure. I should imagine you'll be with us for a few days longer, so that we can keep an eye on you. You know head injuries – sometimes strange things happen. But don't worry. We won't discharge you until we're happy with your progress. Now, I'll go and fetch you some more pills to get rid of that headache, and then if you feel up to it, you can take a shower. A freshen-up will make you feel like a new woman."

~~~~~

Libby couldn't remember the last time she was a patient in hospital, if she ever had been. She wasn't sure, but she had a strange feeling that she had spent some time in a hospital somewhere. Nigel had filled her in about her position as junior ward sister, but his words did nothing to help dispel her anxieties. She couldn't even remember working in a hospital, and when Personnel called in to assure Libby her job would be held open while she recovered, she didn't know whether to be thankful or to cry.

Her last visitor had brought her some joy. Libby thought she recognised the long, lean face of the male charge nurse when he popped his head round the door to her room.

Libby had a puzzled look on her face as she summoned up recognition of her visitor. "I believe I know you – if I could only focus clearer. You're, er…Tim? No, Jim…er, no sorry, I can't quite remember." She looked mortified.

"Don't fret, it'll come. You're nearly there. I'm Jem. I came to see you yesterday evening, but you were asleep. Do you remember picking me up from home yesterday morning? It was very early – before we went sailing."

Libby thought, her brow puckered with concentration. "I remember rain. Yes it was raining, really hard. You got in the car and we drove – where did we drive to?"

"We drove to the Hamble River. We were going on board *Tourbillon*, Nigel's yacht." Jem moved the chair away from the wall and made himself comfortable on it.

Libby shook her head. "Nigel has been to see me, but I remember nothing about being on board a boat, I'm afraid."

Jem gave her a reassuring smile. "Well, I'm sure it'll start coming back once you've had time to get over the shock. What you need is rest. Now, can I bring you anything you might need from home? Do you have your house keys on you?"

"I did have them, but Nigel took them. He insisted on going over to my place and picking up some clothes for me."

Jem looked grim at her words, and fleetingly, Libby wondered why. "Did he now? Well, if you want me to get anything, just let me know. I hope he remembers to feed Rommie."

Libby suddenly gave a wide smile. "I have a cat! And you work in Accident and Emergency. I remember that! Thank goodness! I thought I was never going to get there."

"Bravo! See, as long as you relax, it'll all start coming back. I'll get something sorted so that the cat's fed every day. I was thinking before I came. What if I bring your address book in for you? Seeing a list of names and addresses might jolt your memory some more. I can easily pop over when I sort the cat, and it's not far for me."

"That's a good idea. But Nigel might well have thought of it already. Let me see what he brings over when he visits me again. I can always let you know."

Jem stayed for the remainder of his break and then said he had better get back to work. Libby was relieved, as the longer he stayed chatting with her, the more she remembered. Jem was the catalyst she needed. During his short visit, he reminded her about his own partner, Simon, and various people Libby was friendly with who were mutual friends. After another five minutes or so, Jem stood up and gave her a quick kiss on the cheek.

"I promise to call in tomorrow, but if you need anything urgently or are bothered about something, please give me a ring. The staff here are great, and they'll soon let me know if you have a problem. I'll let Lisa know you've regained some of your memory. She was really worried, and I'm sure she'll soon be down to see you."

Jem's visit had brought some calm and cheer to Libby. She clearly remembered her colleague, Lisa, the senior sister from her own ward and looked forward to seeing her. Libby was also relieved to discover she had a good friend in Jem and, more importantly, one she recognised.

~~~~~

Sitting up in bed, Libby flicked through a magazine that Nigel had thoughtfully brought her earlier. Nothing in the glossy pages enthralled her particularly, and she decided she had made one more discovery. She rarely read magazines and probably enjoyed reading books a whole lot more. Thankfully, her ghastly headache had nearly disappeared, and she felt a bit happier since her shower.

A knock on her door startled her out of her daydreaming. "Come in", she called and sat still as she recognised her visitor standing next to the nurse. She recalled when she had last seen those unusual eyes: deep green and blue and hazel.

"You've got a visitor, Libby. I've told him he's not to stay too long because you're still in a bit of shock. It must be nice to have such a handsome man rescue you," said the nurse, giving the visitor a cheeky smile as she left the room. "I'll leave the door open for some air. It's a bit stuffy in here."

At a loss for words, Libby waited for him to say something.

"Hello there. You probably don't remember me."

"I do as a matter of fact. You're the helicopter pilot. You brought me here."

"I know this is a bit irregular, but I wanted to see how you were. I couldn't stop thinking about you last night. I couldn't come then, but I came as soon as I could. I spoke to the staff, explained who I was, and they were happy for me to visit. These are for you. I didn't know what flowers you like, so I bought a mixed bunch." He looked self-conscious as he produced a huge bouquet of flowers from behind his back.

"Thank you. It really wasn't necessary, but I love flowers and these are gorgeous. I'll have to hide them though because flowers aren't allowed on some hospital wards these days. Won't you sit down?" She indicated the easy chair against the wall.

"I understand from the staff that the blow to your head is giving you some problems?" he asked as he moved over to the chair.

Libby raised a hand to her head, feeling the dressing over her wound. It throbbed, and she couldn't help wincing.

"Sorry. I haven't introduced myself, have I? I'm Rob. Robert Cheesman, helicopter pilot extraordinaire at your service." He gave a slight bow and a broad grin. Despite her position and her predicament, Libby couldn't help smiling back at him. He really did have a nice face, and when he smiled, the skin at the corner of his eyes crinkled into laughter lines.

"You know my name, of course," she said, burying her face in the flowers. "These smell heavenly."

"Sister Libby Hunter, and I'm pleased you like them. But actually, I have a confession to make."

Tongue-tied, she gazed at him. It was unlike her not to know what to say.

"We have met before. It was at a charity party in the city library a month or so ago."

"Really?" Libby frowned while she tried to remember. "I'm sorry. I don't remember it at all."

"Don't be sorry. It was a brief meeting anyway. I was introduced to you, and I was whisked away on an emergency before we could get talking properly. I was off-duty, but this was a high-priority call, and they needed everyone they could muster. I couldn't believe it was you when we picked you up off the boat, what with wet hair and everything. When I saw you last, you had longer hair and were all dressed up." Before she could answer or ask him a question, he continued. "So, how long do they think you'll have to stay in here?"

"I have no idea. I've seen an occupational therapist, and she'll come to see me every day. I've remembered quite a lot now. Every hour things come back to me which is gratifying. You can't imagine how scared I felt when I woke up in your helicopter."

"I can actually. My father suffered from clinical amnesia just before he died. It was so frustrating for him not being able to remember from one day to the next." Robert's voice was soft.

"That's sad. Poor man. I can remember where I live. I know I work here, but that's still a bit hazy, and I can't go back to work yet."

"What about at home? Do you have someone to look after you?"

"No. I live alone." Libby thought about what Nigel had told her. Moving in with him seemed the most obvious thing to do, but was it what she wanted? She considered it was too soon to make such a commitment, especially as she couldn't even remember agreeing to it.

"What about relatives, parents? Any brothers or sisters who'd have you stay with them for a spell?"

Libby shook her head. She felt a wave of misery wash over her. "No, I haven't any – *which* I do remember. My parents were both killed in a car crash, and I have no brothers or sisters." Libby thought for a moment before continuing. "I do have a cousin who lives in Cyprus. But she's got a full-time job on one of the Army bases there, and I'm sure she wouldn't want to be saddled with me."

"What a coincidence. So have I! My cousin Diana is a writer and lives half way up a mountain. I wonder if they know each other, as it's not a very large island. She's coming over in a few days' time to stay. Anyway, getting back to you, we'll just have to make sure you have enough friends to keep an eye on you. I know you may think I'm being presumptuous, but in a funny way, I feel responsible for you."

Libby felt her face grow hot as she flushed in embarrassment. "There's really no need—"

He gave her another warm smile. "I know, but all the same I do. Please consider me a friend. I realise you don't know me from Adam, but I am quite sincere. Look, here is my card and telephone number." Robert dug around in his jeans pocket and withdrew a wallet. "Please keep this. I would be honoured if you let me help you in any way."

"You really are kind, but I couldn't possibly."

"Couldn't possibly what?" asked a voice from the doorway.

"Nigel! You made me jump."

"Couldn't possibly what?" he repeated, coming into Libby's room and giving her a possessive kiss on the lips. Before Libby could register her surprise, he queried, "Darling, who's your visitor?"

Robert stood up and extended a hand to Nigel. "Robert Cheesman."

Nigel ignored his hand. Instead he looked at Libby, clearly waiting for an answer.

"Robert is the helicopter pilot who rescued me. He's come to see how I am."

Nigel visibly relaxed and belatedly offered his own hand in greeting. "Sorry, old chap, but we've been having some odd things happening in the hospitals lately. You can't be too careful who you let in nowadays. Security has been stepped up."

"No, indeed."

While the two men talked above her head, Libby struggled to understand what Nigel meant. She vaguely remembered having a conversation with someone – a male friend, probably Jem, recently about something shocking happening at a hospital, but try as she might, her memory drew a blank.

"You guys do a tremendous job, out in all weather. Thank you for rescuing my fiancée."

Robert looked at Libby as he registered Nigel's proprietary words. "I'd better be on my way. I'm so glad you're getting your memory back, Libby. Take care of yourself and remember: you know where to find me."

Libby couldn't help feeling disappointed as Robert made for the door. "Thank you, I'll remember."

Once he had gone, Nigel walked over to the door and closed it firmly.

"That's better. Now we can have some privacy. You didn't answer my question, my love. What couldn't you possible do, and why did he mention about knowing where to find him? You don't know him, do you?"

For some reason, Libby didn't want to explain her conversation with Robert to Nigel. Robert's card was tucked away in her hand, and she surreptitiously put it under the bed clothes.

"Oh, I can't remember! How silly, and here was I believing I was getting better. I'm sure it was nothing. I don't know why he said that. Perhaps he was being polite." Libby hated telling lies, but if she was honest with herself, she felt annoyed with Nigel. Despite being engaged – and she still didn't feel that she was, somehow – she was her own woman and entitled to talk to whomsoever she pleased. Apart from that, Nigel's manner had been rude when he had ignored Robert's outstretched hand. She slipped the card under her pillow and smiled at Nigel. "Tell me about your day. Have you had a hard day in theatre?"

Chapter 5

As Robert left the ward, he was thinking of Libby. How extraordinary to think that, of all the people in the world, he should rescue her. Ever since that first brief meeting about five or six weeks ago, he hadn't been able to get her out of his mind.

Since then, he had seen her but only from a distance. Before today, he didn't know whether she would remember him, especially as they had only exchanged a few words that first time at the library do. When he had seen her around the hospital at other times, she had been far too engaged in her nursing duties.

Libby interested him, and it was a while since any woman had truly caught his attention. All he needed to do now was to make sure he gained her confidence.

Chapter 6

Summer was at long last upon them. The previous months' bad weather finally heralded in some glorious sunny days with temperatures in the eighties.

Libby was going home today. She was enjoying life once again. She had regained almost all of her memory and felt much happier and more confident than a week ago. She was even ready to go back to work and was looking forward to seeing her old friends again.

Nigel was tied up in London that day, so he couldn't give her a lift home, and Jem was away on holiday in Crete. Nigel explained he often stayed up in London, especially when there was an appointment book full with back to back private consultations at his Harley Street Clinic. Libby didn't mind going to her flat alone and looked forward to rediscovering her home. Her lack of transport hardly mattered, as taxis were plentiful and not too expensive. She found a number for one of the local companies and was just about to ring when there was a knock on her door.

Glancing up, she felt a frisson of excitement go through her. Standing in the doorway, with a ridiculously happy smile upon his face, was Robert.

He took one look at the small suitcase resting on the bed. "It looks like I'm just in time to catch you. Staff nurse said you'd been discharged."

"Hello, Robert. Yes they've decided I'm fit enough to go home."

"That's good news. And what about your memory? Is it all back?"

"Nearly all, some things are a bit murky still, but I'm almost 100 per cent better. What are you doing here?"

Without pausing, he replied smoothly. "I've been visiting someone on the medical ward for some time now, and I thought I'd call in on the off chance you were still here. Lucky for me, wasn't it?" he said, giving her a grin.

She nodded. "Another few minutes and I'd have gone."

"So, how are you getting home? I presume that's where you're going. Is your fiancé coming to collect you?"

Libby thought for a moment. She was certain Robert would offer her a lift home once he knew she was planning on taking a taxi. She didn't know anything about him. He was a stranger and yet, she believed there was something decidedly nice and trustworthy about him. If he suggested he run her home, she could always tell the ward staff on their way out. They knew exactly who he was. After all, it wasn't everyday a helicopter rescue pilot popped onto their ward. "Actually no. He's at his London clinic. I'm getting a taxi."

"Libby, please let me drive you. Save your money."

She dithered. "I don't want to put you to any trouble."

"It's no trouble. I have the day off anyway, and I'm not doing anything else. I said before you could count on me. Which area of Southampton do you live in?"

Libby named the area, and he gave a big smile. "That's on my way home, so it'll be no trouble for me. Come on, it'll save you calling for a cab."

"Thank you, and if it's really not a problem for you, that'll be really great."

~~~~~

On the journey through the Southampton streets, Libby looked around as familiar surroundings flashed past her window. It seemed ages since she had first been admitted to hospital, and she was happy to sit quietly taking everything in. She remembered the route, realising it was the one she took every day for her journey into work. She relaxed and settled back in her seat with a faint smile upon her lips. Nigel was right: she just needed a short while to recuperate, and everything would soon return to normal.

Robert was the first to break the silence. "I've just had a thought. I don't suppose you have any food in the flat?"

Libby shook her head. "No. Only a few tins and packet stuff."

"So how's about we stop off at a supermarket on the way and get some supplies in? You won't feel like going out again later, I bet."

"You're right, but what about you?"

"What about me? My mission today is to get you safely home. But there's no point if you starve to death, is there?"

"I suppose not."

"Right that's settled then. Now would you like to join me in a pub lunch first, or shall we just get you some groceries?"

Libby shook her head again. "If you don't mind, I'd rather just get home. I'm eager to see my place. Thank you for the offer anyway." She felt a bit shy as she made the next suggestion. "If we get something for lunch, we could share it at home. I have a small garden that's nice and sheltered, and we could eat there."

"Sounds good to me. *Al fresco* it is then."

~~~~~

For the first time since her accident, Libby relaxed. It might have had something to do with the half pint of cider

49

that accompanied her salad and rotisserie chicken. Robert's company was soothing too. He was fun, easy-going, and allowed Libby her moments of silence when there was a lull in the conversation.

They were sitting in reclining chairs with the remains of their picnic lying on the table next to them. Libby's cat, Rommie, looked excited on seeing her mistress home again and sat on her lap purring with contentment. Libby was happy to listen to Robert tell her about his interesting work and the foolhardiness of the public.

"You'll never believe half of what people get up to," he said. "I've been called out to all manner of 'emergencies' from sinking boats to people trapped on cliffs with a rising tide to literally hundreds of owners and their motor boats whose engines won't start. They all forget they have a perfectly good anchor and could easily put it down to stop them drifting onto rocks while they take a look at their engine. Some people are completely clueless when they're at sea."

"It's amazing there aren't more deaths in that case," she said, while picking at a small bunch of grapes.

"Yes. But you're forgetting Solent Coastguard has the best pilot around when it comes to safety," he laughed.

Libby joined in his laughter, and as she did their eyes met, stillness falling upon them. They sat in silence, gazing at one another, surprised at their reaction.

"Libby."

"Yes?" she said softly.

"Can I see you again? Would you have dinner with me one night? Tonight or any night you like."

Libby wasn't sure how to respond. She liked this man and enjoyed his company, but what about Nigel? He insisted they were an item. He had given her a ring apparently. She prided herself on being an honest woman. If she went out with Robert what might happen? She could feel there was an attraction between them. She couldn't two-time her fiancé. She felt a telltale flush rising in her cheeks.

As if he could read her thoughts, he carried on. "I realise you're engaged. But I like your company, and there'll be no strings attached. I'm not sure I'm looking for a full-blown relationship anyway. And before you say anything, I'm not one for stealing another man's woman. I promise you."

"It's not that. I do trust you. I'm not sure that Nigel will quite see it that way though."

"Okay. I won't pressure you. But you still have my card, right? Please call me if you change your mind. By the way, is there any chance I could have your number? We're holding an open-day back at the base later in the month, and you might like to visit. I'm not sure of the date, so I could ring you to confirm it, if you're interested?"

"That sounds fun. I'd like to see inside your helicopter from a different position, not lying prone! Hang on. I'll get a piece of paper and jot it down for you."

Libby walked back indoors to find a pen and paper. What was she doing? she asked herself. If Nigel got to know, she was sure he would be insanely jealous. She did have other male friends – Jem and Simon, for instance, but they were partners, and she knew Nigel wouldn't look on them as possible rivals. She decided to stop dithering and made up her mind. She jotted down her home and mobile numbers on a scrap of paper and took it out to Robert.

It was getting late. Hearing the increasing traffic noises on the street outside, she guessed people were already making their way home. Libby didn't particularly want the day to end. She liked Robert. It was a rare thing to feel so relaxed with a comparative stranger. Even the cat was relaxed in his company. She was just about to suggest they had some tea when her doorbell rang.

"Wait there. I'll see who it is," she said, standing up.

Libby opened her door and found a grinning Nigel standing on her doorstep, clutching an expensive-looking carrier bag in his hand.

"Surprise! I had a couple of cancellations. I thought we could have a nice quiet evening on our own or go out for dinner if you prefer, darling." He dropped the bag and wrapped his arms around her and drew her into a long passionate kiss. "Mmm, how I've thought about you all afternoon. London was hellish, and one night away from you is enough. I'm glad I didn't stay for a second."

As they drew apart, he looked at Libby. "You still look a bit pale, my love. I think it better that we stay in, don't you? It's such a pity you won't move in with me just yet. It would be so much more convenient. By the way, I've bought you a present. You can model it for me later." He held up the carrier bag, and Libby read the words '*Mode Sensations*' on the outside.

"Oh, thank you. I'll take a look in a moment, as I was just about to make some tea—"

"Splendid idea. Where shall we sit, in the garden?" Nigel removed his tie and tossed it down on the hall table, already moving towards the open French windows.

Libby lingered just long enough to hear Robert greet Nigel. She didn't wait to hear Nigel's reply, but busied herself making tea. Bother! Despite being pleased that Nigel had made an effort to get back to see her, she didn't know how he would react on meeting Robert again. It was one of the first things she had discovered on regaining her memory; he was extremely possessive.

She pondered over the situation while she laid the tea tray. Well, there wasn't one really. Robert had been decent enough to pick her up from the hospital and bring her home. They had chatted like old friends all afternoon. There was nothing wrong with that. Hopefully, Nigel would see it that way.

"How do you like your tea, Robert?" she asked, setting the tray down on the garden table. The cat was nowhere to be seen. She noticed their leftover picnic and plates. Nigel couldn't fail to notice she had entertained Robert earlier.

"Well, I was about to go actually. Time is getting on." Robert stood up as if to leave.

"Are you sure? Wouldn't you like to stay for some tea? Nigel, I don't know if Robert has told you, but he very kindly gave me a lift home today." She turned her attention to Nigel.

"So I understand. His arrival was most fortuitous, it would seem. I haven't thanked you yet for taking care of my fiancée once again, have I?"

Libby knew from the tone of his voice he wasn't happy. "Robert was visiting a friend in hospital and called on the off chance that I'd still be there. As he was almost passing my door, he offered me a lift." She had done it again! Fabricating the truth where Robert was concerned. She had no idea where Robert lived.

"I see. Well, as I said, it was lucky he found you still there. Have you decided where to eat out tonight? You need to get ready soon, as you probably won't want to make it too late a night. You can wear the new dress I've bought you."

"But I thought you said we'd eat in—" she began.

"There's a fabulous Thai that I know of. Robert, don't let us detain you while we make up our minds where to go. Since Libby's stay in hospital, we have a lot of catching up to do." He broke in on her conversation.

Robert gave Nigel an amused look, and Libby thought she knew what was going through his mind. Nigel was being a pompous ass – possessive and autocratic. Perhaps he was a little too overbearing for her liking sometimes.

"Well goodbye, Libby. Take good care of yourself." He nodded at Nigel and turned to go towards the house.

"I'll just see you out." Libby hurried to catch up with him. Once out of earshot, she whispered to Robert.

"I'm sorry about that. Nigel is…well he's very over-protective. It's just his way, I'm afraid."

"I understand. If you were mine, I'd probably be the same. So long, Libby. I won't say goodbye, as I'm certain we'll meet again," he murmured giving her a kiss on the cheek. "Remember, you know where to find me if you need anything."

Closing the door behind him, Libby leaned against it as she thought for a moment. She was confused. She was with Nigel. He was handsome and charming. He was a top surgeon and apparently came from a wealthy family. All the desirable qualities a woman could wish for. Why did Robert with his warm, hazel eyes make her feel so strange? She would have to put him out of her mind once and for all. Her fiancé, Nigel, should come first.

Chapter 7

Libby couldn't sleep. She tossed and turned for hours, got up, went to the bathroom, made a hot drink, and even read a chapter or two from the book she was reading. She kept telling herself it had nothing to do with the huge row that erupted with Nigel after Robert had left. In her heart, she knew it wasn't true.

After saying goodbye to Robert, she had walked back out to the garden, only to find a fuming Nigel pacing up and down the lawn. Once he realised she had rejoined him, he turned to greet her with a furious expression on his face.

"Can I ask just what is going on behind my back?"

Libby stopped before she reached him with a look of complete astonishment. "Nigel what on earth are you on about?"

"Him!" He waved a hand in the direction of the French windows. "That bloody pilot! Why do I get the impression he's chasing you? Are you encouraging him?"

"No, of course I'm not. And you're wrong on both accounts. It was an innocent lift home. He was visiting a friend and called in on the off chance. He actually said—"

What had he said? Libby tried to remember. *"I realise you're engaged. But I like your company, and there'll be no strings attached. I'm not one for stealing another man's woman. I promise you."* But had he meant it? She also recalled him saying, *"I'm not sure I'm looking for a full-blown relationship anyway."*

"Well? What did he say?"

"He said, he realised I was engaged. He wasn't trying to chase me. Oh Nigel, why are you so uptight? I'm with you, aren't I? The whole thing was perfectly innocent."

"I sincerely hope so. I don't want to come here and find him here with you. In fact, I don't want him anywhere near you. *And* I noticed you've entertained him with lunch." Nigel still looked incensed and agitated.

"It was something simple – a sandwich and a salad. I felt obliged. It was nice of him to give me a lift home. Remember, *you* couldn't. I'm not complaining, I'm just saying. Look, I really doubt I'll see him again. Southampton's a big place. Will you please stop making holes in my turf? Come and sit down and have the tea while it's still hot. By the way, have you seen Rommie? She was here earlier."

"Who's Rommie?"

Libby couldn't help staring. Nigel must remember her. "Rommie, my cat."

"Oh yes, of course. I don't know. I think she wandered off through there." He vaguely waved a hand in the direction of the garden hedge. "Going back to that pilot, he's making a nuisance of himself."

Libby couldn't see why, but refrained from saying so, as she knew it would do nothing to dispel his anger. She held out a hand to Nigel, and he reluctantly moved towards her. Giving a huge sigh, he suddenly pulled her into his arms and held her tight. She breathed in the citrus smell of his aftershave, which was beginning to become familiar.

"Darling, you know you mean the world to me. I just can't bear the thought of another man around you. Promise me you won't be tempted to see him again, innocent or otherwise. I love you so much, and I don't want to share you with anyone. Look – I've got your ring back from the jewellers. Let's see if it fits properly now."

Triumphantly, he produced a small box from his pocket with a flourish. Hesitating, Libby looked at Nigel before she took it from him. With trembling fingers she lifted the lid. Inside, nestling on a bed of gold velvet was a perfect solitaire diamond. She stared at it for a moment. With a deep feeling of dismay, she realised she couldn't recall the ring. She couldn't remember wearing it. Why not?

"Well? Are you going to put it on where it belongs?"

She hesitated. "Nigel—"

"What is it?"

She raised her face to look at him. "I don't know. I'm sorry but I just don't remember the ring at all. Why can't I?"

An irritated look crossed his handsome features. "Darling, we've been through all that before. It's just your memory. Here let me." He took the ring from the box and placed it upon her finger.

"See. It fits beautifully now. It's back in its rightful place. Darling, aren't you pleased?"

"Yeees, I suppose so."

"Libby, whatever is the matter with you? Don't you like the ring? It's a perfect two-carat solitaire. It's worth a fortune."

"I can see that. But I still can't see it belonging on my finger. I feel this is unreal somehow. Oh Nigel, what's happening to me? Why can't I remember?" Libby wailed, putting her hands to her face.

He looked put out. "Stop making so much fuss. I've had the ring made smaller. You could at least look grateful."

Pulling herself together, Libby stared at the ring, wondering why she felt so unsettled and unsure of herself. Was it because she still hadn't completely regained her memory? Without a word, she removed the ring and put it back in the box.

"What are you doing?"

Libby shook her head. "No, it doesn't feel right. I…I'll keep it here in the box until I can remember everything properly. I promise you, once I remember, I'll wear it again." She looked pale and miserable.

"And what if you don't remember everything? What then? Libby, I'm tired of your games today. First I find you entertaining a strange man in your back garden, now you refuse to wear the ring – your engagement ring – I gave you! You wore it with so much pride before your accident. Now you refuse to come and live with me, when we both know it is the simplest and best solution. We haven't made love since you came home. When is all this nonsense going to stop?"

Libby blanched even more at his outburst. The truth was she wasn't ready to climb back into his bed until she could remember how it had been before. She didn't think she had lost her libido but, for some strange reason, something was holding her back. She put it down to her memory loss and tried to reason with Nigel.

"Please, Nigel. Be patient with me. I'm still recovering. It will just take a little more time. You must see that. You're a doctor. Besides, you've said yourself – I need to recuperate."

"Nothing makes sense with you. You keep using that as an excuse now. I'm sorry, Libby, but I've had enough today.

I'm going home – back to my place – where you should be, with *me* by *my* side. I'll see myself out."

He spun on his heel and strode towards the house. Five seconds later, she heard a terrified howl and the front door slamming behind him. Her cat dashed from the house and made straight for her.

Libby sunk down onto the grass as the tears fell. Gathering her cat up into her arms, she began to shake. She didn't want this. She never meant to upset and hurt Nigel. If he could only be more patient and realise how she felt. She was so mixed up inside. She needed someone to talk to. If Jem were here, he would know what to say. He was strong and dependable, but he was away on holiday in Crete. Libby soothed the cat gently and placed her onto the grass. She wiped her tears away with the back of her hand and stood up, clutching the ring in its box. She had to do something physical to stop brooding. Clearing the remains of the picnic away, she thought of Robert. He seemed so solid and calm. If things had been different, she knew she could have called on him for advice and he would have willingly lent her a shoulder to cry on. She was sure that was the wrong thing to do. There had been a feeling, a bond between them, but getting another male involved was definitely the wrong thing to do.

~~~~~

Libby switched on the bedside lamp. It was only five-thirty. She had been awake for three hours! She didn't want another hot drink or a glass of water. She rolled over onto her side and watched the lights from a passing car travel across the mirror on her wardrobe. The door was slightly ajar, and she remembered the dress she had put there just before going to bed.

After Nigel had stormed off, Libby tidied the garden and kitchen. Feeling jaded and depressed, she decided to treat herself to a deep, hot bath. As she walked through to her bedroom, her eyes fell on the bag containing Nigel's present to her. She opened the bag and found a box. Inside, folded between layers of white tissue paper, she found *the* dress. To her horror, it was one of the frumpiest things she had ever seen and completely denigrated the name on the carrier bag, *Mode Sensations*. Whatever was Nigel thinking of? she pondered, as she gazed at the purple creation in her hands. Apart from not being her colour at all, the material was thick and heavy and hardly something to wear during the summer. No one in their right mind would wear a dress with long sleeves and buttoned up to their neck. Libby replaced the dress into the tissue-layered box and shoved it to the back of her wardrobe. It was nothing like anything she would have chosen, and she doubted whether anyone else her age would wear it. Libby felt unsettled over the incident, thinking it showed a dictatorial trait in Nigel that she hadn't noticed before. Hopefully, he would forget about the dress.

She sat up, contemplating what she should do, and her gaze fell on the little white business card lying next to the black jeweller's box containing the ring. Ignoring the box, she picked up the card and read the words printed there.

Robert Cheesman. Mobile 07860 43292. Home 0044 (0)1489 89126.

The home number puzzled her. It seemed familiar, yet it definitely wasn't a Southampton number. It suddenly clicked. The area code was for Bishop's Waltham. That was miles away from inner Southampton! Robert had said that her place was on his way home. It wasn't. It was completely in the opposite direction.

Leaning back on her pillows, she allowed a smile to slide across her face. What a nice man. Despite him saying he had been visiting a friend in the hospital, she suspected he had given up his free day to come and see her and then went out of his way to drive her home. She gave a chuckle. Well, Mr Nigel St John, you might be right. Robert could well be 'chasing her', or he could simply have acted out of kindness. So, should she obey her fiancé or for once in her life act out of character? What if she did see him again? Surely it wouldn't hurt. She would give this matter more thought. Feeling more relaxed, she snuggled down in the bed, rolled onto her side, and fell into a deep sleep.

Chapter 8

A week later, Libby was feeling much better. She was still on sick leave and enjoying lots of free time. Jem was back home and full of talk about Crete, where he and his partner, Simon, had spent their holiday.

That evening, the three of them were to attend an open-air concert in the Royal Victoria Country Park, and Libby was looking forward to it. She had put together a picnic, and Jem was supplying their drinks. Inspecting the contents of the picnic box, she wondered if she had overdone it. There was enough food to feed six people, not three. She smiled to herself. She needn't worry really; long-legged Jem could easily eat his way through at least two people's share of food.

She gave a sigh. Nigel hadn't been invited. When Jem had proposed their evening out, he had made it quite clear Nigel wasn't welcome. Libby was puzzled. She knew Jem didn't have a lot of time for Nigel. He considered him overbearing and arrogant, but why Jem was quite so antagonistic, she couldn't say. Libby knew better. Yes, some people, who didn't know him as well as she did, could be forgiven for thinking him condescending, but that was only show. Nigel wasn't exactly a humble man, but Libby never considered him conceited. When they were alone together, Nigel was kind and very loving – almost too loving, she thought. Nowadays, he was constantly asking her to move in with him, and apart from his possessiveness, she was happy. She just needed a little more time…

The park was situated alongside Southampton Water. It was a popular place for families to spend a day. When the weather was fine, the park was full of people taking a walk, exercising their dogs, or playing a ball game. Watching everyone having fun, Libby found it hard to imagine that this was once the site of the British Army's first purpose-built hospital.

Simon and Jem insisted on picking Libby up shortly after six o'clock, saying it was important to get there in good time to pick the best spot. As they drew into the car park she saw why – it was already over half full.

Simon parked the car and took charge. "Right! We need to be quick to get our favourite spot. Jem, you carry the food and blanket, as they're the heaviest; I'll take the wine; and Libby, can you manage the three fold-up chairs? They're pretty light. If you can't, just say, and Jem'll come back for them. Right, got that? Sorted. Let's go!"

Libby caught Jem's eye and stifled a giggle. Simon was renowned for coordinating Jem, and she too was included in his organisation this evening. Simon knew exactly where he was headed: a favourite grassy knoll that was protected by a large oak tree. Libby hoped the spot was vacant, because she knew Simon would get in a sulk if someone else had dared pitch their belongings on *his* patch.

The chairs weren't heavy, just cumbersome, and after a few paces, Libby trailed behind the others. Within a minute, the two men were swallowed up by the crowd surging towards the open-air stage. Bother! Why couldn't they go a bit slower? Libby thought she had the chairs balanced in her arms, but as soon as she was jostled she ended up dropping them. As she crouched to pick them up, she knew she would have a devil of a job finding Simon and Jem.

"Let me help," said a familiar voice, and Libby found herself gazing into an equally familiar pair of deep hazel eyes. "I never could resist a fair damsel in distress."

"What are you doing here?" she asked.

"Well, I could ask you the same question. But as it happens, I love classical music, especially outdoors in the summer."

Libby stood up and gazed at him, feeling happy and dizzy for some insane reason. He appeared to be alone.

"I saw you arrive, actually. I wondered who your friends were. No fiancé today?"

"No. No Nigel"

Robert lifted one eyebrow – she always admired a man who could do that – and gave her a wicked grin. "Then I'll not be in trouble this time."

Libby smiled back. "What makes you so sure you were in trouble last time?"

Robert gave a laugh. "Well, you didn't see his face when he first walked out into your garden. I felt as if I had tainted your reputation. He's mighty jealous of you."

"It's just his way. He doesn't mean anything."

"So, where is he, your illustrious surgeon fiancé?"

"He's in America. He's the guest speaker at a gathering of world-wide surgeons."

"Hmm. A gathering of surgeons. I bet the collective noun is an incision of surgeons."

Libby gave a laugh. "I've never heard that before. But you're right, it does seem appropriate. Who are you here with?"

"I'm supposed to be meeting my sister and her husband, but I haven't found them yet. Who are your friends?"

"Oh, you mean Simon and Jem? Jem works at Southampton General, same as me. Only he's in Accident and Emergency. Simon works from home. He's a…I don't quite know what you'd call him really. He keeps house for them both and writes poetry and paints."

"I see. Well, we'd better go and find them before they get worried and come looking for you. Where were you headed?"

"Apparently for a large oak tree with a small hillock beneath it. It's supposed to be in this direction." Libby pointed.

"I'll give you a hand, as I'm going more or less the same way." He took the chairs from her and hoisted them onto his shoulder.

"You don't have to, I can manage. What about your family? Won't they be looking out for you?"

"I expect so. If I can't find them, I can always ring Stephanie's mobile. She's bound to have it with her."

They made their way through the crowd, and within a minute, Libby spotted Jem's head towering above everyone else's.

"Jem!" she called. "Over here!"

Jem swivelled his hand round at the sound of her voice and gave a cheery wave of recognition. "Libby, you've got to grow a bit more. Five foot three is not tall enough to get you noticed." He looked at Robert curiously. "Hi, I'm Jem."

"Robert."

Recognition dawned on Jem's face. "Ah! *You're* the pilot I've been hearing all about!"

Blushing, Libby shot Jem an irritated look.

"In that case, I guess I am." Libby squirmed inside hearing the amusement in his voice.

"We're just along here. It's a good spot, as it's slightly raised so you can see the stage without craning your neck, and the tree gives some shelter if it's windy." Jem gave Robert another interested look. "Perhaps you'd like to join us? I'm sure Libs won't mind, and I know Simon would love to meet you."

"That's very kind. I'm supposed to be meeting my sister around here, but there's no sign of her yet. Perhaps I could tag along until I spot her, if that's all right?"

"It's all right with me. Libby?"

"Of course," she murmured. "Why not?"

On reaching their spot, they found Simon had already organised their area. The blanket was spread beneath the branches of the tree and the chilled champagne looked inviting resting in the cooler. Simon eyed Robert a little suspiciously until Jem introduced him as Libby's new friend and rescuer.

"Ooh. We've heard all about you, haven't we, Jem? You must be so brave flying in of those helicopters. Me? I don't even like climbing towers, let alone get up in one of those things. Glass of champagne everyone?"

They all agreed a spot of bubbly was needed to celebrate the occasion – their first outdoor concert that year. Libby sat down in one of the chairs with Robert sprawled at her feet. With less than ten minutes to go before the start of the concert, there was still no sign of his sister and husband.

"They're cutting it a bit fine," he said, when Libby mentioned their whereabouts. "I think I'd better give them a call."

He reached into his trouser pocket and withdrew a mobile. He pressed a few buttons. "Funny. There's no answer. I'll try Graham's number."

A minute later, he looked puzzled. "I can't understand it. They always have their mobiles with them. If there's one thing you can be certain about Stephanie, it's that she will carry her phone around with her. Even into the bathroom, so I'm told."

"Perhaps they're still driving, and they're in a blind spot."

"Mmm. Maybe. I'll give it another go in a minute."

While he was doing this, there was a round of applause as the conductor strode out onto the stage. Once the noise had died down, there were a couple of announcements, and then the concert began. Halfway through the third aria, Robert's own mobile began to vibrate in his pocket.

"Yes, yes. Robert Cheesman. Stephanie Black is my sister…she's what? My God, when? I see…yes…yes…I'll come straight away."

Springing to his feet, Robert captured everybody's interest, the concert forgotten.

"What is it?" Libby asked gently, laying a hand on his arm. His face was completely white.

"It's Stephanie…she's injured…they had a car accident on the way here. A lorry ran into them apparently. She's—"

Alarmed, Libby sat forward in her chair. "Where is she? Southampton General?"

"Yes. I've got to go." He turned in confusion as if looking for the way from the park, dragging a hand through his hair, as if not quite knowing what to do first.

Libby took a split second to decide he shouldn't drive alone. "I'll come with you."

"No, no. You stay and enjoy the concert. This doesn't concern you."

"Yes, it does. You're my friend. You helped me when I needed someone, now I'm going to help you."

"Libby's right, Robert. It's best if someone goes with you. You need some support and company. Shall we all come?"

"Honestly guys, no. I'll be all right."

"Even so, I'm coming with you." Libby stood up, and Robert gave her a grateful look.

"Thanks," he said weakly. "We'd better get moving. Bye fellas."

Simon and Jem shook hands with Robert and wished him well on his sister's behalf.

During the journey to the hospital, Robert looked tense and worried. Libby could only imagine what torment he was going through. After a minute or so, he broke his silence.

"Stephanie is my only sister. We've always got on so well, I don't know if I can handle…"

Libby laid her hand on his arm. "Sssh. Let's wait and see, shall we?"

Robert gave her another grateful look and catching hold of her hand, gently squeezed her fingers. "I really do appreciate you coming with me. I'm not very good with hospitals. Ever since our parents died, I suppose."

"I understand. I think the majority of people who've watched a loved one die feel the same. It can be so hard."

"They never mentioned Graham. Oh God, I forgot to ask! How could I have forgotten?"

"Perhaps he's okay. Surely they would have said something if he'd been injured too?"

Robert gave a huge sigh. "Steph adores him. He's a terrific guy. He's built like the proverbial brick shit house and plays rugby. He's always been more than a brother-in-law, more of a friend really."

He lapsed into silence once more until they arrived at Southampton General. He eased his car into a vacant spot, and they dashed through the Accident and Emergency entrance. After making enquiries, Robert was informed that Stephanie had been admitted to intensive care. Libby thought his face turned even paler as the implications sank in.

"Come on. I know the way," she said, taking his hand in hers. "You'll feel better once you've seen her."

The ITU was fully modernised and equipped. Despite working in a hospital, even Libby waited in trepidation for a staff member to admit them onto the unit. Robert was escorted to his sister's bedside while Libby waited near the unit's office. She knew the staff well and was thankful she remembered everyone on duty by name and sight. Libby decided her memory was almost all back. The only things she was sketchy on were falling overboard and part of her relationship with Nigel, which was strange. She didn't mind too much; things could have been a lot worse.

"So, how do you know my patient's brother then? He's pretty fit by the way," the chatty staff nurse on duty asked Libby with a smile, while they stood outside the ward office. "His face looks familiar somehow. Does he live locally?"

"Not in Southampton, he lives out in the country."

"I just get the feeling I've seen him here before."

"He did have a friend on one of the medical wards recently. He told me he visited them there quite regularly. I'm not sure if the friend is still in here or has gone home."

"Perhaps that's it. He could have used the canteen or something."

After a few minutes, Robert wandered back down to where Libby was chatting with the staff nurse. During their conversation, she had discovered that Stephanie was now conscious and suffering from a broken leg, mild concussion, and some internal injuries.

"The duty surgeon believes she will lose her spleen," the nurse explained. "She's scheduled for surgery later today."

Robert looked worried at this statement. "What exactly will that mean? Can you live without one," he asked.

"Yes. Plenty of people do. There are some complications, however."

"Like what?" He looked stricken.

Libby grabbed his hand. "It's not all bad, Robert. Look, the spleen is a small organ that aids warding off infections by creating antibodies and removing bacteria from the blood. If Stephanie has her spleen removed, there is an increased risk of infection. A person can live a long, healthy life without the spleen. When it's removed due to injury or for a transplant, other body parts, such as the liver or lymph nodes, begin to play a bigger role in the immune system. But as a result of not having a spleen, your body becomes more susceptible to illness. Without a spleen, infections can be deadly if not treated right away. Her physician will probably recommend Stephanie taking antibiotics daily and receiving additional vaccinations.

"That's terrible," he muttered.

"Yes, but liveable-with. If she's healthy otherwise, there's no reason why she can't live to a ripe old age."

He looked down at his feet. "Libby, would you like to come and meet my sister and Graham?"

"Yes, of course, if that's all right with you?" she looked at the staff nurse, who nodded.

"Thankfully, Graham's all right. Can you believe it? All he sustained was some cuts and bruising. Apparently, the lorry pulled out onto the roundabout without looking and ploughed right into them. Steph was nearest to the impact." Robert told her as they made their way to Stephanie's bedside. "Talk about being lucky. Here we are."

"Stephanie, Graham, this is Libby."

Curious eyes were turned to Libby as she contemplated the slight figure lying under the sheet. Libby recognised all the tubes and medical equipment attached to Stephanie and understood Robert's concern. Sitting next to her bedside, was a well-set man. His meaty hands were clasped, holding one of his wife's.

"Hello."

Stephanie's face was thankfully free of cuts. Libby estimated her to be about her own age: thirty-something. She had a pretty face with eyes the same colour as her brother's and long dark hair. Despite her obvious discomfort, she studied Libby with interest.

Graham stood up and took Libby's hand in welcome. "We've heard all about you and your rescue and recovery."

Stephanie smiled wearily. "Yes, a most romantic way to meet my brother. I'm really pleased to meet you, Libby. Robert has done nothing but talk about you."

Robert looked embarrassed and turned to Libby apologetically. "They're making it all up you know. I've only briefly mentioned you."

Graham and Stephanie smiled. "Yeah, only in every other sentence. My wife is pleased that he's finally met someone again who ca—"

"Hey, steady on. We don't want Libby getting the wrong idea." Robert turned to Libby. "Please don't take any notice of them. They're always trying to matchmake on my behalf." He turned back towards his sister. "I forgot to tell you that Libby is engaged – to a surgeon from here as a matter of fact. We are just friends. Okay?"

"We're not here to talk about me. How are you both?" Embarrassed by the personal conversation, Libby moved nearer the bed.

"I'm fine. It's Stephanie who's come off worse."

"Thank you, Libby. I'm okay, a bit uncomfortable. I got a shock when I woke up in here. I'd never imagined I'd end up in ITU."

"You'll be moved into the main surgery ward after your op, I expect." Libby said. "At the moment it's full, which is probably why you're here."

"So they say. Anyway, it's very kind of you to accompany my brother here today. He loathes hospitals. I'm only sorry we didn't get to the concert, and you've missed it."

"It's only a concert, there'll be plenty more," Robert said.

"All the same, we'll go to another one as soon as I'm able." Stephanie stifled back a yawn.

Libby noticed Stephanie was getting tired. The shock and stress from the accident was taking its toll. It was time for them to leave her to rest.

"Thank you for coming. We're so pleased to have met you. As soon as I'm home, Robert must bring you over for dinner one evening."

Robert looked at Libby who nodded in agreement. "That would be lovely. Good luck with your surgery today. You'll probably end up on my ward."

Graham saw them to the door. He was patently worried about Stephanie, and Libby did her best to console him. Despite his size, she could see he was a gentle giant, and dearly loved his petite wife. "I don't know how long she'll stay in, but I promise to make sure my staff keeps a special eye on her if she comes on my ward."

~~~~~

"When are you back at work, Libby?" Robert asked, once they were back on the road.

"I'm not sure, to be honest. At the moment, I'm enjoying my free time at home. Luckily, I have plenty of leave I can use, even if the hospital decides I'm well enough to go back in the next week or so."

"That's good." Robert manoeuvred the car around a cyclist. "Why do they wobble so when you overtake them?"

"Mmm. I always find cyclists scary."

"Thank you for coming with me today. I appreciated your company. As Steph said, I detest hospitals. It's probably after watching my father die."

"That must have been horrible."

"Yes. Not only did he lose his memory, but he had the dreaded big C too."

Libby flashed him a look of sympathy.

"Look, as we've missed the concert, and I do feel guilty about spoiling your fun, how about we go and have some dinner together? I know a great little Italian restaurant not far from here. You must be starving. I know I am."

"That would be very nice, thank you."

He gave a laugh, and Libby asked him what was so funny.

"Well, it seems despite your fiancé's efforts, I am going to be allowed to take you out to dinner after all and without any manoeuvring on my part! Sorry, I'm being mischievous. I'd like to see his face though. He would not be amused."

Libby smiled, but a small niggle of doubt crept inside her. What if Nigel returned home early? He didn't even know she was supposed to be with Jem and Simon that day. She shrugged. It was her life and not his. She never knew what he got up to when he was away on business, and there had to some kind of trust between them. "Italian is one of my favourites."

Chapter 9

Robert surprised Libby with his knowledge of food. The restaurant he had chosen was almost hidden down one of the back lanes of Southampton, and Libby certainly wasn't aware of its existence. As they entered the establishment, the owner greeted Robert like an old friend, and she knew instantly that Robert was a frequent patron of Alfredo's.

Alfredo slapped Robert on the back with affection and then turned his black, beady eyes upon Libby. A delighted smile greeted her as he took in her elfin looks and slim curvy body.

"Signorina, I am delighted to meet you. But Roberto, she is bellissima! Where have you been hiding this bella donna? It is a long time since you brought a beautiful girl to my restaurant" Alfredo bent over, and his lips brushed her hand. "For you, I have the best table," he whispered in her ear. "Discreet and secluded where no one can spy on you for your little romantic dinner, eh?" He beamed at them and indicated they follow.

Libby was amused at the little man's antics and caught Robert's eye as they sat down. With a flourish, Alfredo whisked the crisp white table napkins onto their laps, handed them menus and then proceeded to tell them about 'tonight's specials'.

"I have the special tagliatelle coi gamberi e asparagi, vongole in porchetta, and agnello alla siciliana. To start, may I suggest the Ligurian minestrone and to finish crostata di mandorle. I'll leave you to look at the menu, and then I'll be back for your order. A drink to start with, perhaps an aperitif?"

Libby knew little Italian and was thankful that Robert knew his way around the dishes. He consulted the wine list and ordered a classic Chianti, once he knew Libby preferred red wine.

"Robert, you'll have to help me, as I don't know much about Italian food apart from the usual pasta dishes. What do you suggest?" she whispered once they were alone.

"Alfredo was suggesting the minestrone soup to start with. How hungry are you?"

"Famished actually."

"Okay then, we'll start with that. I've had it before and it is delicious. You have a great choice of pasta, and all of it is made on the premises. The specials were, let me see...ah, here. He mentioned tagliatelle with prawns and asparagus, clams with herbs and wine, and Sicilian lamb. Personally, I love his trenette al pesto di noci, that's pasta with walnut pesto. Trenette are typical of the cuisine in Liguria, which is where Alfredo comes from. For dessert, he suggested almond tart."

Libby rolled her eyes as he explained. "It all sounds so fabulous. Decisions, decisions!"

"I'm going for the lamb, I think. Starting with the soup, then lamb, and if I've room, the tart.

Libby looked through the menu again. "I'll take your recommendation and try the walnut pesto, as I've never had it before."

Happy with her choice of dishes, Libby took time to look around the restaurant. The restaurant was almost full. When a woman entered and quietly asked for a table, Alfredo graciously showed her to one a little distance away from where Robert and Libby sat. With the glowing light from the flickering candles, Libby couldn't make out the woman's features. She only knew she was slim and blonde and obviously enjoyed red wine. *That could be me sitting there on my own,* Libby thought.

Alfredo poured the wine, and they sat back savouring the bold, dry and full-bodied Chianti while waiting for their food.

"This is a delicious wine," she said after a few tentative sips. "As I mentioned earlier, I know nothing about Italian food or wine. Of course, I've been to quite a few restaurants and cheaper pizzerias, but this place is rather special."

Robert nodded in agreement. "Alfredo is unique in Southampton. His father started the restaurant when he first came over from Italy. Alfredo was just a babe in arms then. Anyway, he eventually followed in his father's footsteps, and now we have the best-kept secret in the city. I come here a lot."

"I gathered as much. Do you cook much at home?"

"Yes. I have to feed myself. Besides, I get a lot of enjoyment out of it. What about you?"

Libby gave a sigh. "I'm not very good, I'm afraid. I never seem to have enough time to open a cookery book and make something different, let alone special. I make do with simple things like grills or one-pot meals. Did you teach yourself how to cook?"

"I did. Your grills and one-pot meals are okay. Not everyone has the inclination to spend lots of time in the kitchen. I just happen to enjoy it when I'm at home." He looked reflective while telling her this, and she wondered if he had ever shared a kitchen with someone, someone who was close enough to matter.

There was a pause before he continued. "Of course you can always come round and try my cuisine," he said giving her a mischievous look.

Libby smiled and relaxed. "You are naughty. You know how I feel about two-timing Nigel. Mr Cheesman, our relationship must be purely platonic – you know that and you promised."

He looked sheepish. "I did, didn't I? I must have been mad to agree to those terms."

She raised her eyebrows and gave him a warning look.

"Okay, okay," he laughed, holding up his hands in mock penitence. "I give in. I promise. But the invitation holds. I'd love to cook for you some time. Really I would."

"I'll think about it."

"As you're smiling, I know you'll capitulate eventually. No woman can resist my chocolate mousse!"

Their soup arrived, and they tasted Alfredo's masterpiece in silence.

"This is amazing," said Libby. "How can he make something to taste so wonderful with just a few diced vegetables?"

"Ah! It's all in the secret ingredients. I've begged him for years to tell me, but he never budges. Wait until you taste the next course. You'll be a convert for life."

"I'm already converted."

"So tell me why you're working here in Southampton and not London where you trained?" he asked as he laid down his soup spoon.

Libby thought for a moment. "It was Jem. We met in London on a course. We sort of clicked as friends, and I mentioned that I liked sailing but never had the opportunity living in London. When the position of junior sister came up, he let me know, and I applied for it. It seemed like a God-given chance to work near the sea and in a major hospital."

"I see. And Nigel? I presume you met him at work too?"

Libby nodded as she finished her last mouthful. She wiped her mouth on her napkin and continued. "Yes. He's one of the consulting gynaecological surgeons, and we sometimes have one or two of his cases on my ward. We started going out together—" She stopped. When did they start going out together?

"Yes?"

"Sorry, I was trying to remember how long we have been going out. Some things are still a little fuzzy. Yes, it must be about five or six weeks now."

"And already you're engaged? He must be one fast worker."

Libby wrinkled her nose while she fiddled with the stem of her glass. "Yes, he must be. We hit it off, I suppose."

Robert looked at her curiously. "You suppose?" he said softly.

Libby met his gaze. "I didn't mean it to come out like that, and this will sound a bit strange to you. Nigel and I have a great relationship. He's extremely kind and loving. He gets a bit uptight sometimes, but that's just his way, and he's very protective of me. But—"

"But what? Does he make you laugh?"

Libby thought for a moment. "He's quite a serious person; but yes, I'm sure we share lots of laughter together."

"You don't sound very sure," Robert murmured. "You learn to like someone when you find out what makes them laugh, but you can never truly love someone until you find out what makes them cry," he quoted.

"Robert, don't."

"Don't what? It's just a quotation. I don't know where from, but I've always liked it. But going back to Nigel. You said just now that 'this will sound a bit strange'. What exactly did you mean?"

Libby looked embarrassed as she fidgeted in her seat. "Well, we are engaged, but it's strange—"

"Yes?"

"I don't actually remember being engaged. What I mean is, I can't remember actually getting engaged. It's a complete blank."

"I see. Maybe it's one of the last vestiges of your amnesia. I expect it'll all come flooding back to you soon."

Libby looked unhappy and tense while twiddling her wine glass around in her fingers. As the waiter approached their table, Robert broke the tension. "Ah, it looks like our main courses have arrived."

~~~~~

Robert was right. The food was excellent. They finished eating and relaxed over coffee. The conversation turned to a familiar topic – sailing – and Libby was surprised to find that Robert owned his own sailing yacht.

"Of course, it's nothing like you're used to after sailing on Nigel's super beast, but I love her."

"Why have you never mentioned you had a boat before?"

"The occasion never arose, I guess."

"What's she like? Is she a modern yacht or an old wooden one? Where do you keep here?"

Robert laughed. "Hang on! Give me a chance to answer! I think she's beautiful. She's modern, thirty-eight foot long, and I keep her on the Hamble River in a marina."

"Fabulous! Can I see her?"

"Of course. Just let me get the bill and we'll go."

Libby laughed. "I didn't mean now, silly."

"Why not? It'll only take us a matter of fifteen minutes or so if we take the back roads. Come on, it's not as if you have to go to work tomorrow or have to get back home early. You're mistress of your own time. Live a little, Libby," he urged with softness in his voice.

Libby felt unsure. She was intrigued with Robert. He was constantly surprising her. She had finally relaxed, but was aware of the subtle undercurrents that ran between them. What if…darn it! She could do what she liked. Robert had just said she was her own mistress.

"Okay. Just a quick look then," she said and gave him a shy smile.

~~~~~

'Caterina' was gently bobbing with the oncoming tide. She sat securely in her marina berth with her mast rising tall and stately against the blue-black sky. A tangy breeze blew in from the open sea, and Libby took a deep breath enjoying the smell and taste on her tongue.

She bent down to remove her heeled shoes and accepted Robert's helping hand as he guided her on board.

"Welcome aboard *Caterina*."

Libby wandered over the teak deck, noting where everything was kept, while Robert watched her with an amused smile upon his face. He remarked how he loved keeping a tidy boat. Libby agreed and noticed all the ropes neatly coiled and the cockpit smelling fresh and clean. Below, she marvelled at the snug but modern saloon.

"She's gorgeous and has that wonderful smell of a new boat," she exclaimed in delight.

"Well, she's less than a year old, and I take great pride in maintaining her."

"Can I look round?"

"Of course you can. Would you like coffee or a glass of wine?"

"Mmm. Not sure. What are you having?"

"Coffee. I have to drive you home, and if I drink any more, I'll be well over the limit."

"Okay, I'll join you in that case."

"Do you feel okay going on a boat after what happened last time?" he asked from the galley.

"Fine thanks. Nigel said it was an accident, due to that foolhardy Sebastian. Apparently, he came too close, illegally, and Nigel had to gybe to avoid him. It's a lucky thing we didn't collide or others might have been hurt. Thanks." Libby accepted the steaming mug of coffee and sat down on the upholstered bench settee with her legs curled under her. Looking around the saloon, Libby noted how every piece of brass and woodwork gleamed. The made-to-measure furniture was elegant and traditional. Overall, the boat looked classy without being too obvious and flashy. *Caterina* 'felt' like a well-loved and cherished yacht, and Libby was completely at home on her. "She really is lovely. When do you sail?"

"Whenever I get the chance. I'll probably take her out tomorrow as I have a day off."

"Nice."

"Want to come?"

"I'd love to, but some other time maybe."

"What's wrong with tomorrow? When is Nigel due back? He need never know."

Libby laughed. "You really are incorrigible you know! Nigel is due back on Monday."

"So what's stopping you then?"

She wagged a finger at him as if to say *you know why not*. Robert sighed in mock drama fashion and gave her a grin.

"Coward."

"I am not!" She laughed, laying her coffee mug down on the table.

"Then prove it. Come along tomorrow. The weather forecast is good. We can call in and see Stephanie afterwards, if you like."

She was tempted. A day out sailing might be just the thing to blow away the cobwebs. She wondered why she felt a bit depressed and decided it was because she was missing Nigel.

"Okay, I will. But you'll have to take me home soon, or I'll never get up in the morning. It's getting late and I'm feeling rather tired."

"We could actually stay the night on here, you know. There are two cabins."

Libby didn't need to answer, her look said it all. Robert gave her another cheeky grin and placed their empty mugs in the galley sink. "Okay, time to go home."

Chapter 10

Libby felt alive as she stood at the helm of *Caterina*. She was a joy to handle and responded with the lightest of touches to the wheel. Robert said she was a natural sailor and was happy to work the winches and handle the sheets while Libby stood behind the wheel. They had a wonderful morning tacking up and down the Solent, and with lunchtime approaching, Robert said it was time to head back to the Hamble River if they wanted to visit Stephanie later. Once they had taken the sails in and started the engine, Robert produced a couple of baguettes filled with tasty ham and chutney.

"That was scrummy. I didn't realise I was so hungry."

"It's the sea air. It never fails to give you an appetite. Fancy a cuppa now or shall we wait until we're back in the marina?"

"I'm happy to wait."

There was little traffic going their way as they motored up the river estuary. Most were going in the opposite direction. Robert took the wheel once they entered the channel proper, and Libby stood on the deck gazing at the craft moored in the passing marinas.

"Where does Nigel keep his boat then?" Robert asked.

"At Port Hamble. We'll pass *Tourbillon* in a moment. See the tall mast on the hammerhead pontoon? That's her."

"*Tourbillon* means whirlwind in French, did you know?"

Libby nodded. Standing on the side with the wind blowing through her hair, she felt tremendously happy. She had loved her morning sailing with Robert, who had proved to be the perfect companion. He was so easy to talk to and made her feel good. He was always ready with a quick joke, and Libby found herself laughing that morning at the silliest of quips.

"There she is!" she called out to Robert. "I wonder who that is—" Her words dried as she recognised the figure in the cockpit. As her voice carried over the water, the figure turned towards her. With a feeling of horror, she realised just who it was standing there. As she looked into his eyes, she felt his fury.

~~~~~

"I know you think I'm crazy, but I've got to go and see him and explain."

"Explain what, Libby? That you've just spent a very nice four hours sailing up and down the Solent with a *friend*? And what about Stephanie? Aren't you coming with me after all?"

Libby thought for a moment. "I'd better not. Nigel will be livid if I don't go to meet him. He'll want to know what I've been up to."

"And what about him then? I thought you said he was due back tomorrow not today?"

Libby looked miserable. "He must have finished the meeting early. I'm sorry, Robert, but I feel so guilty…I should have switched my mobile on, But I forgot I turned it off during the concert. If I'd put if back on afterwards, then I would have known he was home. He would have telephoned me."

"Well, he didn't leave a text message, did he? Libby, there's nothing to feel guilty about. Why do you persist in feeling guilty? He went away and left you here on your own. He can't expect you to sit at home all day, can he?"

Libby didn't answer because that was exactly what Nigel would have wanted. He would have expected her to wait by the telephone until he rang.

"Okay, I'll give you a lift back to Hamble Point. But for God's sake don't apologise to him. We've done nothing wrong." He looked and sounded extremely exasperated.

"I know that, you know that. You have to understand something, Robert, and that is Nigel is under a lot of strain at the moment. He has such a responsible job, and the pressures that come with it are huge."

"We all have responsibilities, Libby. My own occupation is not all a bowl of cherries." He caught the obstinate look in her eye and held up his hands. "Okay, okay. I get the message. I'll drive you back to him. Just don't expect me to coming running when—"

"When what, Robert? Were you going to say, when we're finished? Is that what you think? Nigel and me won't make it together? Oh, very funny! Well let me tell you something. Nigel is kind and honest, and I can't see him throwing his attention onto someone else's fiancé. I think we better cool it right here and now. I'll get a taxi – no, don't bother. I never want to see you again. You can keep your blessed boat." She shouted. "I'm off."

"You're mad, do you know that? Throwing yourself at him. I've seen his sort before. Libby, I'm telling you, he's not the one. Trust me."

Libby was out of the cabin and already half-way across the cockpit. "Oh really, and now you're going to tell me that you are, I suppose? Well, I wouldn't want you if you were the last person on earth. Goodbye!" she spat back at him.

Chapter 11

Robert watched as Libby clambered over the side rail and jumped down on to the pontoon. Without another look in his direction she ran off towards the marina office where he knew she would find a list of taxi numbers.

Damn the man! And damn her! Just when he thought everything was going so nicely. Robert was sure Libby enjoyed their day together – like she had obviously enjoyed last night in Alfredo's. Robert had planned a nice family visit to see his sister. That would have convinced Libby of his honourable intentions, and he felt sure he could easily have persuaded Libby to spend more time with him afterwards.

He was surprised at her reaction. Sure, she was bound to be nervous where Nigel was concerned. He came across as a real power freak and totally possessive. Robert was more furious with himself when Libby had seen Nigel on his deck – he should have made sure she was below fixing a coffee or something, and it was his own fault for not discovering for himself where Nigel kept his boat. He was usually a much more careful planner. Another mistake like this, and he would have blown his plans – and he did have plans – and Libby featured very highly in them.

Chapter 12

While she was in the taxi, Libby went over and over the dreadful scene with Robert. Whatever had possessed her to say such awful things? She wasn't normally so rash and impulsive, but he had riled her so. Dratted man. She pushed him to the back of her mind as the cab approached the entrance to Hamble Point marina. What was she going to say to Nigel? How would she explain her morning with Robert? Thankfully, she didn't have to mention their dinner together last night. She felt sick inside as she paid the driver his money, not noticing his grin when she told him to keep the change. It wasn't every day he was given a large tip, especially on such a short journey. With a feeling of despondency, Libby began walking slowly towards *Tourbillon*.

Nigel was nowhere to be seen on deck. Not wishing to anger him further by going on board without his permission, she rapped timidly on the hull. Her mind was whirling in confusion while she waited for him to appear. When he did, she found she was tongue-tied.

"Well, are you going to come on board or not? Or have you had a better offer today and are here with some feeble excuse?" he asked with an icy note in his voice.

Libby removed her shoes and climbed onto the yacht. "Can I just explain?" she began before he interrupted her.

"Libby, I'm not interested in your excuses. All I know is I saw my fiancée with another man. One who's been doing his best to steal you away from me. Can I ask you something? Are you sleeping with him? Because you certainly don't want to sleep with me just lately. I'm at my wit's end with you, Libby. Just what are you playing at? Why are you acting so cheap?"

Libby gulped in horror at his suggestion and stammered as she answered him. "No, of course I'm not. Nigel, I'm *so sorry* not to have been here when you returned. If you'd only rung me or left a text message, I'd have joined you at once. I wasn't expecting you."

"Ha! Obviously not. And do you mean, give you some notice?"

"Nigel! Listen! Robert means nothing to me. He really is just a friend. If you'll let me explain—"

"Libby, do you really expect me to listen to more of your lies? I know what I saw. You were with another man, and it wasn't the first time. Yes, I did try to telephone you last night but got no answer from your mobile. Neither could I make contact this morning. Little did I know that my darling fiancée was off having fun with someone else."

"My mobile was turned off because I went to a concert with Jem and Simon. Later, I just forgot to turn it back on as I was in the hospital. I promise you, it's the truth. You can ask them if you like."

"Humph. What were you doing at the hospital? And when did you organise your little jaunt with whatshisname around the Solent? Or was that another coincidence, him just turning up out of the blue?" he scoffed.

Libby muttered that this was the case, knowing full well that it sounded as lame to her ears as it must have to Nigel's.

"Nigel – I don't know what to say to make you believe me." To her horror her eyes began to fill with tears. Within seconds her face was streaming.

He gave an exasperated sigh and handed her a hankie. "Do stop dripping all over the deck. You'll ruin the teak. You'd better come below. I don't want to spend the rest of the afternoon up here with all and sundry looking on."

Libby sniffed, wiped her face and followed him down the companionway into the saloon.

"Sit down." Nigel indicated one of the settees. His face was cold as he studied her. "Would you like a drink?" he asked, holding up a bottle of white wine. She nodded and tried to smile, wishing everything to be right between them.

She never considered she was a weak female, but she loathed scenes and dreaded falling out with boyfriends.

Nigel disappeared into his cabin, and Libby sat down upon one of the saloon settees. *Tourbillon* was huge compared to Robert's *Caterina*. Not only was she a bigger yacht, she was swankier too. As much as she admired Nigel's racing yacht, Libby discovered that she actually preferred Robert's smaller more intimate boat.

Nigel returned to the galley from his cabin and turned his back on her as he uncorked the wine and got out a couple of glasses. There was silence while he poured the Chablis and passed a glass over to Libby. She took a couple of sips and discovered the wine was enjoyable. Hating the silence and not knowing how to break it, she drank most of it down in haste, as it gave her something to do. Nigel topped her glass up before even taking a mouthful from his own.

After a tense few minutes, he finally spoke. "As far as I'm concerned, there's only one solution to this."

Libby wondered what he was thinking of. Was he going to suggest they split up? A slight dizziness came over her, and his voice seemed to be waver as if from a distance. She sat more upright in an attempt to pull herself together. She did feel odd; she felt really dizzy now, almost as if she was wading through cotton wool. Concentrating, she gave him her best attention.

"You'd better move in with me as soon as possible. That way I'll know you're definitely mine and no one else's. We can be together whenever I'm down here."

Libby felt her tears welling up again and a lump in her throat. Whatever was the matter with her? She was never this emotional. She struggled to be rational and decided she didn't deserve Nigel. He was so good to her. Relieved he seemed to have forgiven her, she nodded her answer. Libby didn't notice his triumphant look as Nigel realised he had achieved his goal. He sipped his wine while watching her from the galley. Libby buried her face in her glass while finishing her drink.

Libby suddenly felt weak and sleepy. Her eyelids fluttered as she lifted her head to say something and yawned instead. She was stupid staying up late with Robert last night. All she wanted to do now was lie down and go to sleep.

Placing his glass on the galley worktop, Nigel walked over to Libby and pulled her into his arms.

"Libby, you don't know what this means to me," he muttered into her hair. "We'll be so happy together, okay?" Without waiting for an answer he crushed his mouth to hers, leaving her breathless and weak-kneed. Her limbs felt so heavy and leaden. Without another word, he swept his arm under her legs, picked her up and carried her into his cabin. As he snatched her clothes from her, Libby found she could hardly keep her eyes open and shivered in anticipation. She was vaguely aware as Nigel stripped off his shirt and fumbled with his fly, and then with a cry of triumph he flung himself down upon her.

Hours later, while Nigel was sleeping, Libby felt around the bed for her clothes. She still felt odd: dizzy and disorientated, it was almost like she was drunk. She dressed, and stole up onto the deck without disturbing him. The late evening was a promise of a beautiful day tomorrow. Libby saw nothing of it. Confused, she allowed her tears to fall. She sensed she and Nigel had made love. She was sore and bruised between her legs, but try as she might, she couldn't actually remember having sex. She remembered nothing about his body, his kisses or his lovemaking. Perhaps the strangest fact of all was she *never* remembered making love with him – *ever*.

Libby had a sense she had sealed her own fate somehow. She couldn't remember, but she got the impression she had agreed to do something. She loved him, she was sure of it, but she still had this feeling of needing more time. What was she going to do?

Chapter 13

Libby felt happier when she returned to work. Since her argument with Robert, she found herself questioning all her thoughts and actions. By throwing herself back into her duties on the busy surgical ward, she had little time to dwell on her problems.

Personnel made good their promise and the senior sister on her ward, Lisa Williams, made sure that Libby didn't overdo the heavier work.

"It's not every day you get knocked out and lose your marbles, is it?" she joked, while they were sitting in the ward office discussing their patients. "If you have a relapse, they'll blame me. So light duties for you, my girl." She held out a packet of chocolate biscuits to Libby. "I've got a real taste for these all of a sudden."

Libby smiled at her colleague and friend. "No thanks. I hardly think I'll have a relapse now. I'm fine, don't fuss so. You're worse than Jem and his Simon." The mention of Simon and his precious ways had them both giggling.

"Don't." Lisa laughed. "He cracks me up sometimes. I never know how I keep a straight face when he's around. Thankfully, he doesn't work here. He'd never survive."

"You're telling me. Anyway, he hates the sight of blood. He faints if he has to have a blood test, so Jem says."

"Love works in mysterious ways," Libby said.

"And what about you then? "

"What about me?"

"Jem told me in confidence that you and Nigel St John just might be an item."

Libby cast a quick look round making sure no one was within earshot. "Hush! We want to keep it secret. Wait until I get hold of that Jem! He knew he wasn't supposed to tell anyone yet."

"Well, I've heard it now. Jem, bless him, says he was only thinking of you. Since you're now back at work, he said I should know because we work so closely together. Anyway, Libby, why all the secrecy? Most people newly in love want to shout it from the rooftops, especially with a catch like Nigel St John. He's got to be the most desirable male we've had around here for years. With his sexy good looks, even I might have been tempted with a fling."

"It's Nigel's idea. He doesn't want his ex-wife to get to hear about it."

"Why ever not? If she's his ex, what's it got to do with her? She works abroad doesn't she? America, isn't it?"

Libby shrugged, "Yes. New York and London, I believe, although I hear she's going to spend a year in Sydney soon."

"She's a lucky girl, with all that travel. Are they actually divorced?"

"Yes, of course, Nigel said he received the decree absolute ages ago."

"That still doesn't explain why he wants everything between you kept a secret."

Libby shook her head, caring neither way. She had no parents to tell about her newfound love. If she was honest, she felt a bit depressed about it all. She had always dreamt she would meet someone, fall deliriously in love with them, tell the world about it, and get married. At the moment, nothing seemed settled.

"It's what he wants."

Lisa peered at her. "But is it what you want, my dear? Are you happy with him?"

Libby pulled herself together and flashed Lisa a huge smile. "Yes, of course. And I'm fine. Really I am. I'm just a little tired, and Nigel relishes his privacy. Don't forget, Nigel has been under a lot of pressure this last year since taking the post on the Trust board."

"Mmm. He has been ever since that nutter attempted to kill him. Do you remember the man? He tried to bring a case of malpractice against Nigel at his previous hospital, and then he laid in wait for him one night after his appointments were finished. Nothing ever came of it I believe. I wonder what really happened. The press never got hold of the true story. Nigel was lucky there wasn't a scandal. All too often these days, people point the finger for the most trivial of things, and the awful thing is they often get away with it. There's many a doctor who's suffered from someone with either an overactive imagination or simply by telling lies about them."

"I don't know. He's never mentioned any of it to me, and it's none of my business. Lisa, how do you know all this? You never cease to amaze me with your capacity for gossip! All I know is he's very hardworking – too hard most of the time – and he's very caring towards his patients."

Lisa gave a shrug. "I'm sure he is. Anyway, hospitals always seem to attract the nutcases for some reason. You've heard about last night's horrible scare, haven't you? There's been another sighting of that stalker again. I'm glad I don't work nights." She gave a shudder.

Libby gave a horrified gasp. "Really? No, I didn't know that. What happened and where was it?"

"Apparently, last night around two, a midwife had to go to the blood bank and she stopped to have a quick cigarette break outside beforehand. She was approached by some man wearing a dark coat. She had a fright when she thought he was about to expose himself to her but had the foresight to run back to where there was more light. Apparently, he attempted to corner her, but when she kneed him in the crutch, she was able to get away."

"Did she say what this man looked like?"

"No. It was too dark. All we know so far is she said she thought he was white, quite wiry and slim and possibly wearing some sort of wig, but apart from that nothing else."

"Scary. Remind me not to volunteer for any nights either."

"Mmm, it must have been very frightening, especially coming after those two nurses going missing earlier in the year. I was hoping we'd seen the end of that ghastly episode, and St Thomas's Hospital is having its own problems I see. What is the world coming to? I put it down to far too many graphic films and novels these days." She gave a huge sigh before continuing. "Anyway back to you and Nigel. Surely you'll let your friends know you're seeing each other soon? Think of all the parties you'll miss out on if Nigel doesn't want to go?"

Libby nodded. "We'll get round to it, I'm sure. Maybe we'll have a party ourselves once I move in with him."

"That'll be fun. I'll look forward to it. Right, it's four o'clock now, time for the drug round. Would you like to do the honours this time?"

Libby nodded her assent and took the drugs cupboard keys from her. She always enjoyed the drug round as it gave her a chance to chat to the patients and ensure they were comfortable. With so much paperwork these days, getting to know the patients was almost a luxury.

Stephanie had been sent up to her ward, and Libby found her easy-going, just like her brother. She knew from her delicate questioning that Stephanie was aware of Libby and Nigel's argument and Robert's involvement, but she never directly asked what the row was about. Now Stephanie had been discharged, complete with a carrier bag – or so it seemed – of antibiotics and painkillers, and she made sure Libby had her address and telephone number.

"Don't forget, I'm inviting you to supper as soon as I'm back on my feet and feeling more like myself," she said as she left the ward on crutches. "It'll probably be in a week or so."

Libby sighed, not wanting to dwell on Stephanie or her brother. The truth was she missed Robert with the laughing hazel eyes. She missed his easy wit and banter and the little smiles he had given her when they had shared dinner together on *Caterina*. Why did life have to be so difficult?

While Libby was pushing the drug trolley round the ward, she noticed Nigel in the office. Lisa was with him, and Libby presumed he was there checking up on his theatre cases. With the hospital full, they had had to take a couple of emergency gynaecological patients. Nigel had already been on the ward twice that day, and Libby couldn't help admiring him for his care. Not many consultants took as much trouble, she mused.

When they had finished the drug round, Libby returned the trolley to the office and locked it. She discovered Nigel had left the ward and thought it a bit odd that he hadn't made any attempt to speak to her. Sometimes she thought he carried all the secrecy about their relationship a little bit too far. Shrugging to herself, she decided to go and tidy the linen cupboard. They were waiting for a delivery of clean linen from the laundry, and now was a good time to sort the shelves out before the new bundles arrived. It was an easy task and undemanding. Just as she finished, she heard a movement behind her and found the doorway blocked by one of the porters. She knew the porter, as he was a regular visitor to their ward, and Libby recalled his name was Peter. Peter was in his late thirties. He was pale and thin, with a mass of untidy dark hair. Libby also recalled that he was incredibly shy, especially with women.

"Peter, you gave me a start. I didn't hear you come in. Have you brought our new linen up?"

Peter stared intently at Libby without saying a word. Instead, he directed his gaze to the scar on her forehead, which she had attempted to cover with her fringe. Without a word, he grimaced and pointed to her head and then to his own.

Libby wondered what he meant and frowned. "What?"

"I have one too," he muttered. He brushed his thick hair to one side, and Libby saw a deep puckered scar along his hairline. However it had happened, Libby saw it must have been a severe injury.

Libby nodded. "Yes, you have."

"Did your mother do that to you too?"

Libby almost gasped at his statement. "What? No, of course not. I had an accident. Don't you remember, Peter? I was hurt on a boat, and I've been off work while it healed."

Peter remained where he was with a puzzled look upon his face, as if he was slowly turning her words over in his mind.

"Peter, I need to get out of here now. Can you please let me pass?"

He remained where he was. His mouth trembled, as if he was working out what to say to her. Libby suddenly felt vulnerable as he took a step nearer to her, his hands stretching out towards her. For some strange reason, she felt the urge to scream and backed away until she was pressing up hard against the shelves behind her.

"You need to take more care when you—" he began.

"Peter, what are you doing?" Lisa's voice came from behind. "You know you're not supposed to be in there."

He gave Libby another look and then turned round in the doorway giving Lisa her first view of her.

Lisa frowned and took his arm. "Peter you need to unload your linen trolley. Come on, let's get it cleared. We need it."

As he followed Lisa back out onto the ward, Libby found she was shivering, and she hurried past them into the sister's office and sat down.

"Are you okay? You look like you've seen a ghost," Lisa said once she had rejoined her.

Libby lifted her pale face and nodded.

"What did he say? He didn't…he didn't do anything, did he?" Lisa frowned. "He's never been any trouble despite his wild looks. Peter's always been a gentle sort of fellow; very shy and introverted though. He has Asperger's Syndrome and finds it really hard to fit in socially. He has the classic triad: lacking social communication, interaction and imagination."

"No, he didn't do anything. I think he just surprised me, and I got a bit spooked. He started saying something else, but I didn't quite catch what he said."

Lisa breathed a sigh of relief. "Good. I'd hate to have to report him for something. It must be hard to get a decent job when you're as inhibited as he is. Are you sure you're okay now?" She peered at Lisa. "What about a nice cup of tea? I'll make it."

"Yes. No, I'll make it. I need to do something. I'm just being pathetic. I think it was because we were talking about that stalker earlier. Not that I suspect him or anything, it was just me being silly."

"Well, if you're sure then. Peter really is harmless. He spends a lot of his time here in the hospital. I'm told he has a sort of social life. He belongs to a local drama group. He doesn't act of course, he's too unsure of himself, but he helps with scenery and then there are his trips up to London. Apparently, he loves hanging around Waterloo Station watching the trains come and go. A few of the other porters reckon he's looking for someone. It's most probably his mother, who was a manic depressive and hanged herself. Peter was found sitting next to her swinging body four days after she took her own life. Poor little kid – he was only about seven at the time."

Libby gave a gasp of astonishment. "The poor man! What a terrible thing to witness, especially as a child and your own mother! That's enough to turn anyone's brain."

"Yes, it is. Except poor Peter isn't mentally handicapped. If you manage to get him talking on a subject that he knows about – and I doubt anyone could since he's so reserved – he'll amaze you with his knowledge. It's almost as if he has a photographic memory. There was some story about his mother inflicting some injuries on him when he was a little nipper, but I don't know how true that is."

Libby nodded as she took in all Lisa was telling her. Peter *had* mentioned his mother. He had asked Libby if her own mother had caused the scar on her forehead, like his mother had done to him. She took a deep breath and stood up saying, "I think I'll make that tea now. After what you've just told me, I think we need it."

Chapter 14

Peter was confused. As he walked back along the long corridor towards the canteen, he thought about the little blonde sister on the surgical ward. Not the older chubby one, Lisa, the other pretty one; the sister who had the red scar on her forehead, just like his own. He was confused because she said she had had an accident. Peter didn't know when she had had her accident, but that wasn't the point.

No, Peter was confused because she looked a lot like the nurse from last night, the one who had got away from the stalker. She too was small and wore her blonde hair short.

Chapter 15

At the end of the following week Libby found herself with the whole of the weekend off. It was rare to have both days clear, and she wondered what to do with her free time. Nigel surprised her when he had let slip that he needed to go back up to London for an emergency meeting. He had already left the day before. Libby thought, if only he had let her know earlier, she could have gone with him. It was ages since she had visited the capital, and a weekend would have been exciting. They could have taken in a show and gone to one of Nigel's favourite restaurants for dinner. When she had mentioned it, he had sounded regretful, saying that he wouldn't have time to accompany her anyway as his meetings were back to back and sure to run into the evening. They hadn't seen too much of each other that week either as Nigel ran a couple of very full clinics right up to the weekend.

"Sorry, Libby, this emergency meeting has just landed in my lap. I promise I'll make it up to you at a later time."

"Okay, it doesn't matter really. I have plenty to occupy myself with, and the garden needs tidying."

Libby didn't mind too much because it gave her time to herself, and with him being away, there was no reason for her to move into his apartment. He must have read her mind as his next words were rather startling, "Why don't you start thinking about what you're going to bring with you when you move in with me? You'll need to have a clear-out you know."

Libby was a little disturbed, as she had never considered getting rid of any of her belongings. Many of the things scattered around her flat once belonged to her parents, and although not valuable or even particularly nice to look at, they were all that remained to remind her of them. She was noncommittal with her reply, simply saying she had inherited her parents' furniture and treasures, and she would sort a few things out for the charity shop.

"You know, there is no real hurry over this. It's not as if we're getting married yet. I can easily leave my flat as it is and sort stuff anytime. I've been thinking about moving in with you, and I really believe we should have a trial run first. Maybe I can stay over for just one night a week until we know we're really compatible. I've never lived with anyone else before, and I'm finding it a bit strange. Please understand Nigel, you must realise this. You've been married and lived with your wife."

When he had hung up on her rather abruptly, she guessed she had annoyed him.

~~~~~

Libby decided not to spend any more time in bed, even if she was enjoying the novel by Lia Fairchild. She would have a shower and a leisurely breakfast for once and then go into town. Stephanie had rung her earlier during the week and invited her to a party.

"Graham and I invited a few friends over, and before we knew it, we had enough people for a full-blown bash. I do hope you can come."

"It sounds great. I haven't been to a party in ages and it gives me an excuse to buy something new to wear. What time does it start, and can I bring anything?"

"Any time after seven will be good and just a bottle. Graham has arranged all the catering from outside, so I don't have to lift a finger. Wasn't that considerate of him? By the way, I shall expect you to bring your fiancé with you. I'm dying to meet him."

Nigel seemed reluctant to go at first, saying he had a lot or work on, but he eventually agreed. Now, of course, he was in London, and Libby was going on her own. She had been in two minds about it. Robert was bound to be there, and since their argument, she hadn't seen or heard from him. She felt embarrassed since that last time together and realised she had overreacted. Robert was owed an apology, and she wasn't looking forward to it.

She gave herself a stern talking to and decided she was being incredibly 'wussy'. Robert was a nice man, and he would most probably accept her apology gracefully. As far as she was concerned, it would be a shame if he didn't, but it was hardly worth worrying about.

After checking the weather, Libby decided she didn't need a jacket. For once, it promised to be a glorious day. The BBC weatherman had declared a sunny and dry weekend the night before, and this augured well for Stephanie and Graham's party that night.

Libby unlocked her car door and inserted her ignition key. The engine sounded sluggish at first, and Libby thought back to when she had last had it serviced. It was well overdue, but after a minute or so of idling, the engine revs picked up. Libby backed out of her drive.

Traffic was light, so she arrived at West Quay in good time. She enjoyed the lively atmosphere around the waterfront, and decided to sit in the sun with a coffee before tackling the shops. It was fun watching the world go by while sipping her cappuccino. As she was about to leave and head for the shops, she recognised a familiar face in the crowd. Robert was walking along the quay.

With a jolt, she realised he wasn't on his own. By his side was a striking, long-legged woman pushing a child's 'buggy'. The way the woman smiled at Robert and then laughed at something he had said, told Libby this was no casual girlfriend. The woman was probably older than Libby and visually stunning. She had shoulder-length reddish-brown hair, and her sundress showed off her tanned and slim body.

Libby frowned as she looked at the woman. There was a sense of intimacy between them, and Libby felt a pang of disappointment. Watching their apparent friendship, Libby experienced a real feeling of being alone. With alarm, she realised Robert had noticed her as she gazed in their direction. He was sure to come over and say 'hello'. Whatever was she going to say to him? She needed to apologise for her over-the-top behaviour the other day, and it wouldn't be easy in front of a stranger.

As they drew nearer, Libby almost squirmed in her seat. To her embarrassment, as she lifted a hand in greeting, Robert took the woman by the elbow and guided her and her child away in another direction.

Libby felt as if she had been slapped in the face. How rude! She knew he had spotted her at the table. They had been just feet away, and yet he had deliberately chosen not to stop, not to even say a polite 'hello'. She felt her face flame. She got up hurriedly and went into the restaurant's ladies' room. Once she had rinsed her face and hands, she stared at her image in the mirror. The face that looked back at her was pale and tense. She noticed dark smudges under her eyes, and it looked as if she hadn't had a good night's sleep for weeks. She wondered who the red-haired beauty was and was shocked to find she was jealous. The more she thought about it, the angrier she became.

During the previous few weeks Robert had made it quite clear he found her attractive. Although he had given her no more than a passive goodnight kiss, he had been very charming. He made no bones about fancying her, and she definitely felt a spark between them. She was sure she hadn't misunderstood the signs. Because she was with Nigel, she had deliberately pushed Robert away. Now she saw that she had been horribly mistaken. Robert was in no need of her affection. He already had one woman in tow.

With a flash of anger, she snapped her handbag shut and left the room. Well, Mr Helicopter Pilot, she needed none of his advances. She had seen him in his true colours, and didn't feel guilty anymore.

Libby made her way to the shops and went into the most expensive women's clothing shop she could find. She was going to buy the most gorgeous and daring dress ever. That would show him.

Chapter 16

The watcher couldn't understand her attitude. With the others it was so easy. They were all so lonely and eager to comply as planned. As always, the watcher took every precaution to be especially careful; and then, this one would be the last. There had been four so far, and the journey was almost over with just one more to go. The watcher enjoyed living this *alter ego* and found that an understanding and love of amateur dramatics was greatly beneficial.

Having selected her, the watcher now had to make sure the victim was ready. The watcher couldn't wait for the victim's fate to be joined to Amy's, whose body, weighted with stones, rested beneath the Thames River; to meld her story with that of Elizabeth's, whose bones were rotting in the ancient woodland of Hampstead Heath; with Gemma, forever sleeping in the New Forest just west of Southampton; with Susan, sleeping peacefully in the salt-marsh thick reeds of the shores of Dibden Bay; with all these sisters of death.

In the meantime, the watcher would carry on having some fun. The other hospital girls were light relief until the final hand was in play. They had done nothing wrong, they were just nursing staff. As far as the watcher was concerned, they were fair game.

There was plenty of work still to be done before she was fully compliant, and the watcher didn't want to make her suspicious. She would make this mission complete, and the watcher would finally be at peace once she was told, *you're mine, all mine.*

Chapter 17

Stephanie and Graham's party was in full swing when Libby arrived. She was a little late, as her Mini was still playing up. It needed a few minutes to warm the engine, and once she was under way, she became caught up in heavy traffic.

Their house was in a leafy suburb of the city, and with the fine weather, most people were enjoying the evening sunshine out in their back gardens. Stephanie was holding court from her chair on their patio as Graham escorted Libby over to her, and they exchanged hugs. Stephanie looked well, and no one would have known about her recent car accident but for her plastered leg.

"Libby! I'm so glad you made it. You look gorgeous! Where did you find that dress? But where's that fiancé of yours? Don't tell me you're on your own?"

Smiling, Libby sat in the spare seat next to her, wondering which question to answer first. "I'm sorry, but Nigel couldn't make it after all. I'm afraid he has an urgent meeting in London. He sends his apologies and hopes your party is a success. I bought the dress today in The Wardrobe in West Quay. I'm pleased with it too."

"It really suits you and is so daring. I'm not sure I'd have either the figure or nerve to wear it!"

Libby laughed. "Yes, it is a bit risqué, isn't it? Between you and me, I wasn't too sure if it was a tad too much, but the saleslady was very persuasive."

Libby's dress was a figure-hugging sheath of green jersey with a deep low cowl neckline at both the front and back. She had spent time over her make-up and hair and the effort showed. She looked beautiful.

"So how are you? You look well, I must say."

"I feel fine. The leg plaster is a bit of a pain, especially when it comes to having a shower, but I put a waterproof covering over it, and I can manage okay. Graham's being wonderful. He does all the difficult household chores and makes me sit down. He does draw a line at ironing though. I've found I can manage quite well sitting down to do it, especially if I can watch a film at the same time. Mind you, I swear I'm putting on weight with the lack of exercise. As for you, you look positively skinny."

Libby nodded and smiled, but she wasn't giving Stephanie her whole-hearted attention. She knew that Robert must be here somewhere. She cast a quick look round the other partygoers but didn't recognise anyone.

"Sorry, what was that you said?"

Stephanie took a sip of her Pimm's before replying. "I said it was too bad that Robert might not be able to make it tonight."

Despite that morning's shock on seeing Robert with the gorgeous red-head, Libby felt her heart sink. She gave herself a mental shake. What was the matter with her? He was nothing but all talk and probably a womaniser as well. "Oh? And why is that?"

"He didn't say, just that he might be tied up this weekend. I know he's not duty pilot, so it's probably something to do with his boat. You, of all people, should know that a man's yacht is always his first priority. What's the common phrase among sailors? Something about 'first lady' I believe." She laughed, not spotting Libby's lukewarm reaction.

"I see." Libby knew with whom he would be tied up. Suddenly, the life seemed to go out of her. She felt tired and listless. With Nigel away too, her weekend was proving to be one big disappointment.

Stephanie peered at her. "Libby are you all right? You look a bit pale."

She smiled at her hostess. "I have a slight headache. I'd better go easy on the alcohol. It's probably the weather."

Stephanie looked doubtful but nodded. "Mmm. I'm only allowed one drink and a weak one at that. Mind you, I can't say I miss it all that much."

Graham wandered out from the house and asked Stephanie if he should start letting people have some food. He smiled at Libby and complimented her again on how nice she looked.

"Can I help in any way?" she asked, standing up. "What about handing round plates of canapés?"

Graham paused. "Well, if you don't mind. I was going to do it all by myself because the caterer is up to her neck in the kitchen. Yes, if you're sure, that would be a big help."

Grateful to have her mind taken off Robert and what he might be doing, Libby followed him back into the kitchen.

A delicious aroma greeted them, and Libby could see that the caterer had her hands full. "They're plated up and ready to go out to your guests," she said as Graham eyed the food laid out on the pine table.

"Libby, meet Pauline, cook extraordinaire!"

The two women smiled at each other and Pauline indicated which plates Libby was supposed to hand round.

It was a great way for Libby to get to meet everyone, and the next couple of hours flew by. She made sure everyone had enough to eat and managed to snatch a dance or two.

She forgot how many glasses of Pimm's she had drunk. By twelve o'clock, her feet ached in her high heels. She felt decidedly tipsy, and she was beginning to flag. With a sigh of pleasure, she eased her feet out of her shoes and sank down into an easy chair. Graham brought her a plateful of delicacies and a glass of champagne.

"Here you are, love. You've earned it. I don't think I could have managed without your help. Cheers!"

Libby took an appreciative sip and smiled at him over the rim of her glass. "I'm sure you'd have found someone else."

He grinned. "Maybe, but not from anyone as pretty as you. You did a grand job. Stephanie's grateful too. By the way, I've just had a call from Robert saying he'll be here in a short while."

He gave her a grin. Libby didn't know what to say. From the look on his face, it appeared Graham knew nothing about her row with Robert. As Stephanie hadn't mentioned it, Libby decided Robert must have kept it to himself. Graham wandered off back outside leaving Libby to finish her meal. Suddenly she felt trapped. He would be bringing that gorgeous creature with the perfect hair and body with him. Libby made a decision. She had experienced one episode of Robert ignoring her and didn't want another.

Putting her unfinished plate of food down on a table next to her, she hastily swallowed the glass of bubbly and stood up, brushing crumbs from her dress. If she was quick she could say 'goodbye' to Stephanie and Graham and get out of there before Robert arrived.

As she looked round for her handbag, she felt a draught from the front door, and turning, she found the subject of her misery looking thoughtfully at her from the doorway. Peering round him, Libby noticed he was alone. Tongue-tied, she didn't know what to say. Should she ignore him and leave or try and brazen it out?

The decision was taken from her as Robert made the first move. He made as if to turn around and go into the garden, then he stopped and walked over to her. Libby felt her heart thumping in her chest as he approached.

"Robert," she murmured, noting he looked like he had cut himself shaving.

"Libby. I just want to say, because this is my sister's homecoming party, I don't want to make either a scene or let her know the truth about our falling out. I—" He paused as he dragged a hand through his hair.

"I'm sorry," she mumbled.

"What?"

"I said I'm sorry. I'm sorry about that day on *Caterina*. I said some awful things, and I wished I hadn't. I never meant them."

Robert stared at Libby, trying to make up his mind whether he believed her or not. Libby hesitated. She felt sick inside and, for some reason, on the verge of tears. She had just apologised, and he hadn't made any comment. She attempted to walk past him when he grasped hold of her arm.

"Do you mean that? Are you sorry?"

Libby's lip trembled, but she spoke in a firmer voice. "I said so, didn't I?" She took a deep breath. She mustn't let him think she cared one way or the other. "I had no right to say any of those things. Please let go of my arm, Robert, you're hurting me."

Robert's eyes darkened and Libby thought he clearly didn't believe her.

Her heart pounded and her mouth was dry. Libby rushed towards the kitchen, thinking there would be plenty of people there to talk to. She moved towards the group hanging and laughing round the bar. She needed a drink badly.

"Libby, what can I get you?" Graham asked. "Would you like some more champagne, or would you like another Pimm's?"

"Champagne! After all, we're celebrating Stephanie's recovery. Thank you and cheers to everyone!" Libby forced a note of gaiety into her voice after raising her glass to the others. There was a chorus of well-wishers. Libby could see

Robert in the corner of her eye as he followed her into the room. Glass in hand, she continued through to the garden.

Her earlier seat next to Stephanie was occupied, and Libby looked round in panic. She really wanted to leave. She was determined to say her goodbyes there and then. She had had more alcohol than usual and was in danger of becoming drunk if she stayed.

"Are you going? Oh, what a shame. Still if you have to work, then I do understand. Libby's a sister at Southampton General," Stephanie declared to the couple sitting near her. "She gave me wonderful care when I was on her ward." The others looked over to Libby with interest and soon found she was fending off questions concerning the so-called watcher or stalker, as he was now called. Being a member of the hospital staff, all the guests seemed to think she had some inside information. However, once they realised she knew little more than they did, they soon joined Stephanie in saying 'goodbye'.

Libby and Stephanie agreed to get together during the week, and Libby was able to escape by the front door after locating her shoes and handbag.

As the door shut behind her, she drew a deep breath and steadied herself. She felt dreadful. Meeting Robert and behaving like a coward, she didn't deserve to feel otherwise. She walked down the drive towards the direction of her parked Mini, wobbling dangerously in her high heels. Drat! She realised she had definitely had far too much to drink and was well over the legal limit. She would have to be ultra-careful once she got behind the wheel. She knew she should call a cab, but her first priority was to make a quick getaway from Robert.

She took a deep breath, attempting to sober up, and took a moment to look around her while she remembered where she had parked her car. Having arrived late, the spaces near Stephanie and Graham's house had all been taken, so she had parked further down the road. It was a couple of hundred metres, and Libby set off along the path. At first, she imagined the figure moving stealthily between the trees on the other side of the road. When she finally realised she wasn't alone, she panicked. She fumbled in her handbag looking for her keys and ended up dropping them. After scrambling around on the pavement in terror, she managed to retrieve them and insert the correct one into the lock. Terrified, she felt nausea beginning to wash over her as she saw the figure getting closer…

If only she hadn't had those last two glasses of champagne, she thought. She turned the key in the ignition. *Please start, please start,* she prayed. The engine was sluggish and backfired as she pumped the accelerator. Why on earth hadn't she had the damn thing serviced? she remonstrated with herself, almost sobbing with fear. She turned the key again and waited – nothing happened. She was petrified as she sat there, not knowing what to do. *Lock the doors,* she thought. She turned in her seat towards the door knob and went to press the button down, God, she felt so woozy and sick again. Perhaps she…

A tap on the glass made her scream. She looked up and saw Robert next to her car, bending down at her window.

"Whoa, why are you so jumpy? Are you having trouble? What seems to be the problem?" he asked, speaking through the window.

"Robert! God, you gave me a fright. It won't start. It's been playing up lately." Her heart was thudding in her breast.

"And when did you have it serviced last, eh? Don't tell me. Women seem to have this uncanny knack of waiting until something goes wrong before they decide to do something about it, even if it means their vehicle might be dangerous. Come on get out while I have a go."

Feeling foolish and unsteady on her feet, Libby half climbed, half fell out of the car. He supported her once she stood up.

"Bloody hell, how much have you had to drink?" he grumbled. "There's no way you should be even attempting to drive home. Come on, I'll take you back."

Libby tried to stand up straight and didn't succeed. Instead she slumped against the car and slowly began to slide down.

Robert wasted no time. He hoisted her upright and put a supporting arm around her. "My car's just down here."

"No, no," she said weakly. "I don't want—"

"What you want and what you're going to get are two different things entirely. You are in no fit state to either drive or argue."

Putting an arm around her waist, he marched her down to his car, pushed her into the passenger side, and fitted the seat belt around her before climbing in himself. Once he was seated, Libby began to moan.

"Don't argue, Libby. Just shut up will you? I'm driving you home, and that's final."

"I said, I think I'm going to be sick!"

Muttering an oath, he reached over and opened her door – not a moment too late.

Chapter 18

Libby opened her eyes and groaned. Who on earth had a road drill going today? Being a weekend, surely it wasn't allowed. She gave a start. Where the devil was she? Struggling to sit up she stared at the room she was in. She was lying in a double bed in a room with walls painted a soft green. There were long curtains covering the windows, and a wide wardrobe and tall chest of drawers stood against another wall. For one terrifying moment, Libby thought she had lost her memory again, but when she felt how raw her throat was after being sick earlier, it all came flooding back. She remembered leaving Stephanie and Graham's house and getting into her car – which wouldn't start! Robert! Robert had been there. She gave another groan. It didn't take a huge amount of imagination to realise she was in Robert's house. She had another thought – she sincerely hoped it wasn't his bed!

She threw the bedcovers off and discovered she was only dressed in her underwear. She couldn't recollect taking her dress off, but where was it? Libby stood up, crossed over to the curtains and drew one aside. She found she was looking down onto a surprisingly pretty and cared-for garden. Neat hedges and well-cut grass competed with a couple of colourful and well-stocked flower beds. Her head swam, and she realised she was suffering from one hell of a hangover. Her throat was parched, and she would have given anything for a glass of water.

A slight tap on the door had her whirling round in the direction of the sound. Embarrassed over her state of undress, she hurried back to the bed and pulled the covers over her. Seconds later the door opened a crack, and Robert poked his head in.

"Good morning. How's the hangover then?" he said cheerily.

"Terrible."

"Fancy some tea?"

"Lovely."

"Milk, sugar?"

"Just a spot of milk please."

"Hokey doke. I'll be right back then."

Libby could hear him whistling somewhere in the house. Nursing her sore head, she lay back upon the pillows wondering just how on earth she had managed to land herself in so much trouble. Sometimes life wasn't fair.

"One cup of tea." Robert tapped on her door again before stepping inside.

Libby sat up making sure the sheet was up to her shoulders and then felt foolish as she was sure it was Robert who had removed her dress and shoes before leaving her to sleep off the alcohol. Drat the man!

"I expect you're wondering where your dress is?" He indicated the wardrobe door, and Libby nodded as she took a sip of tea.

"Sorry, but I couldn't let you drive home in the state you were in last night. And if I'd taken you home in your car – if I'd managed to get it started – then I'd have had no way of getting back here. I doubt if you'd have liked finding me asleep on your sofa in the morning either." He grinned ruefully at her.

"But it's okay for me to wake up here, is it?" Libby asked softly.

"Don't be scratchy! Look, it was the best and probably the only thing to do. Oh, I suppose I could have taken you back into Stephanie's, but you were so out of it, it was unbelievable. At least this way nobody need know you spent the night here. If I'd spent the night at your place, I expect your fiancé would have found out somehow and beaten my head in. We both know how paranoid he is."

Libby caught her breath and exhaled with a deep sigh. "I suppose so. How did you—?" She indicated her state of undress.

Robert nodded. "Yes, but I averted my eyes – honest." He gave Libby a cheeky grin. "I thought it best because you might have been sick on it again or ruined it in bed. It's okay, anyway."

"Thank you for going to so much trouble. I seem to be repeatedly in your debt somehow."

"Libby I—" He stopped. "Oh nothing. Look, get up when you want to. I'm not doing anything important today, and you can lie in for as long as you want. When you feel like it, I've got some nice fresh rolls and coffee for breakfast. Take your time. The bathroom is just along the corridor on the right, help yourself to a shower. There's everything you'll need in the top drawer of the chest here, including towels."

With that, he turned on his heel and left Libby nursing her cup of tea. He hadn't misused his power over her, and she felt completely at ease in his house, in this bed, even if it wasn't directly his. Robert never ceased to surprise her.

~~~~

After showering, Libby tidied the covers on the bed and, carrying her ludicrously high heels in one hand, made her way downstairs. A gorgeous aroma of warming bread and freshly-brewed coffee met her once she reached the ground floor. Following her nose, she found Robert sitting and reading in the kitchen.

"There you are. Sit down…please. Coffee or more tea?" Robert got up and laid his newspaper down on his seat.

"Coffee, please." Libby moved over to the table and sat down opposite where he had been sitting. As he busied himself with the coffeemaker, Libby leant over and picked up the paper. Within seconds her attention was caught by the headline in the local rag. *'Nurse violently attacked at Southampton General!'* Libby gasped as she read the text, a feeling of horror creeping over her.

So what Lisa had warned her about was all true. There definitely was a serial stalker at the hospital, only this time he hadn't just given someone a fright, he had viciously attacked one of the nurses. Libby read on, *'During the early hours of Saturday morning, Staff Nurse Eloise Black was savagely attacked as she stepped outside the hospital building during her break. Ms Black was admitted to the hospital and is said to be suffering from multiple stab wounds and severe shock. A police spokesman said, 'we are treating this case with the utmost severity and welcome any person or persons who may have witnessed or have some information about this shocking attack. All information will be treated with the maximum confidentiality.'* There was a contact name and police telephone number at the end of the article.

Libby didn't know the staff nurse, but that hardly made any difference. This poor woman had been subjected to a brutal attack while on duty at the hospital. Libby looked at the report again, but there was nothing else written on the subject. *Multiple stab wounds!* She looked over at Robert with a stunned look upon her face.

"Yes, I've seen it. Terrible isn't it?" he said. "Do you know her?"

Libby shook her head. "No, I don't. But then I've only been there a year, and it's a big place."

Robert nodded and placed a mug of coffee in front of Libby. He indicated a jug of frothy milk and the sugar bowl already on the table. "I wonder why hospitals seem to attract so many weirdoes."

Libby shrugged. "Maybe they don't. Maybe it's just that there are so many people in one place all at once. I knew we had a stalker, but this is one step further. This is dreadful. And it happened last night according to this," she said, waving the newspaper in his direction. "I do hope she'll be okay."

"Do you ever work nights?"

"Not if I can help it. Sometimes, when we're really short. I haven't done any for months now."

"Well, for God's sake, please don't if you can avoid it."

Libby was surprised at the urgent tone of his voice and met his eye. "I'll do my best, I hate working nights anyway. They always mess up my body rhythm."

Robert turned away and walked over to the oven. Wearing oven mitts, he removed half a dozen golden crusty rolls and placed them in a basket. "Do you think you could manage to eat something?" he asked, putting the hot rolls in front of her. "I always find lining your stomach with something makes a hangover pass more quickly."

Libby eyed the hot bread. It did smell good, and wanting to please him, she put a roll onto the plate in front of her. "I'll try. I still feel a bit queasy, and my head aches."

"You'd better have some water then, too." Robert filled a glass. "Drink that before the coffee and then eat," he ordered.

Libby gave a small smile at his bossiness and drained the glass. "Aye, aye Captain sir."

"So where is the illustrious surgeon boyfriend this weekend then?"

At first, Libby ignored Robert as she fiddled with her breakfast. Knowing that he wouldn't let Nigel's absence remain unexplained, she laid her knife down with a sigh.

"Nigel had to go up to London. It was something to do with his last meeting there. He didn't really have time to explain to me in detail."

"Uh-huh. Goes there a lot does he?"

Libby frowned as she thought about Robert's question. "Quite a bit."

Robert bit into his roll and chewed as he watched her playing with a jar of honey.

"Wasn't he married before?"

"Yes. How did you know that?" She spooned some of the honey from the jar and watched as it dripped onto the bread.

"I can't remember where I heard it. Maybe it was when Stephanie was in hospital or...no, I remember now. It was Jem."

"*Jem?* When did you see him?" Libby's knife clattered on her plate when she dropped it in surprise.

"I ran into him last week. We like the same pub down in Hamble Village. I'd been doing some work on *Caterina* one evening and popped into the pub for a drink before going home. He was there with Simon. We had a couple of pints together."

"Ah, I see." Libby said, taking a tiny bite of honeyed roll. She thought it was a bit odd that Robert should bump into Jem. As far as she knew, Jem and Robert had only met the once, at the concert when Stephanie had her accident. If anything, she was surprised they had even recognised one another.

"He said that your Nigel had been married before to another doctor. Apparently, she works in the States."

Libby nodded. "Yes, she spends part of the time in New York and London. She's a psychiatrist." So they had been discussing Nigel and most probably her. Jem was a real old gossip at times.

"So, when is he returning home?"

"I'm not sure, he didn't say for definite. I only know he's going to be away for the whole of the weekend." More questions! Libby flashed him an irritated look.

Robert finished his roll and reached for another. "Come on, Libby, eat. You'll feel a lot better, I promise you."

"Okay, I'm sorry to be so slow, these are delicious."

"When you feel up to it, I'll run you back to your car, and we'll try and get it started. I suggest we take it to a garage to get it looked at. There's one round the corner, not far from where Stephanie and Graham live. I've used them before. They're thorough and not unreasonable. Is that okay with you?"

"But I can't have you going to loads of trouble on my account. I know I should have had it checked out ages ago. I can get a taxi…" Her voice trailed away, knowing somehow that Robert would never leave her to deal with her problem car on her own.

"Libby."

"What?"

"Stop talking. I'm sorting it for you and that's that. I bet you haven't taken it for a service for months. If only you women knew how dangerous neglected cars can be. I assume you never check the brakes or the tyres? The simplest of tasks too! Do you know the five cardinal rules for looking after your car?"

Bemused, Libby shook her head. She could feel a short lecture coming on.

"Well first, keep an eye on your brake pads. If you neglect your brake pads and shoes, your brakes will ultimately fail. Secondly, change the oil. Oil is the lifeblood of the engine. As a nurse, you should know all about that! Then there's the air and fuel filters which need changing regularly, and finally, replace your headlight bulbs when they burn out. Oh, and of course, good tyres with plenty of tread.

"Now come on, finish your breakfast. When you're ready, we'll get going." He glanced at her clothing and gave a cheeky grin. "That dress you're wearing may be okay for a party, but it's definitely a no-no as far as the garage is concerned. I wonder what the boys there will think!"

~~~~~

Libby's car needed at least a full day's work and the garage manager promised he would do his best to let her have it ready some time on Monday. Robert and Libby wandered back to Robert's own car. Once seated, he asked Libby if she needed to be run anywhere else that morning.

"No, I don't think so, thanks for asking though. I really should be..." Libby's voice trailed off as her attention was held by a silver Porsche Cayman S which had stopped at the traffic lights. Robert followed her gaze and then turned to Libby with a quizzical look upon his face.

"What's the matter?"

For a moment, Libby didn't answer. When she did, her face had paled. She slid down in her seat below the dashboard.

"That's Nigel's car. I recognise the number plate."

Robert swivelled his head round. "And if I'm not mistaken, that's the man himself. I wonder who that is with him." He glanced back in Libby's direction with an almost accusatory look. "I thought you said he was away until at least after the weekend?"

"I did. I wonder why he's back so early. I hope he hasn't seen me. You know how jealous he can be."

"Not just jealous, downright unreasonable if you ask me. No, he's not looking your way. You can come up now the lights have changed."

Libby sat up straight and cast a tentative look towards the road. "Sorry. I just didn't want another scene. I know you've got me out of a hole today, but Nigel can be irrational, like you just said."

"Well, let's get going anyway. Luckily, we're going in the opposite direction. How's the headache now, Libby?"

"Nearly gone, thank you."

They drove the rest of the way in comparative silence, each lost in their own thoughts. Libby was still wondering what Nigel was doing back in Southampton, when he had quite definitely told her he would be in London for the whole of the weekend. None of it made sense. Neither did the last time, when she had gone sailing with Robert, and Nigel had spotted them as they motored up the Hamble River. If she didn't know better, she might have suspected he was seeing someone else. Libby thought it highly unlikely in view of how often he had asked her to go and live with him. She suddenly realised what Robert had said earlier, about seeing someone in Nigel's car. She hardly dared ask if the person with Nigel was male or female. She was sure she knew what the answer would be.

As they pulled up outside her flat, Libby couldn't help having a quick look around to make sure Nigel was nowhere to be seen. Robert must have read her thoughts, as he gave her a roguish grin.

"It looks like it's safe. Your fiancé is nowhere in sight."

Libby gave him an apologetic glance. "Sorry. I know he was going in the opposite direction to us."

"Come on, that's not all that's worrying you, is it?"

"You'll no doubt think I'm daft, but I just have this horrible feeling that I'm being watched sometimes. I'm sure it's because we've been talking about that awful attack on that poor nurse, and I'm probably being paranoid, but I haven't felt that everything is as it should be since I came out of hospital. And on top of everything else, I'm feeling a bit low. Depressed is too strong a word for it, but I honestly don't feel right."

Robert looked worried as he listened to her words. "Have you seen your GP? It may be a backlash from your accident, the depression thing. Look, I know you won't want me to suggest this, but I'd like to check that everything is all right in your flat. It'll make me feel better knowing you'll be okay. Can I come in and make sure all the doors and windows are secure. At least then you can sleep safely at night. Are you the only key holder to your flat?"

"Yes. I've never given one to anyone, except—"

He flashed a look at her. "Except?"

"Oh, it's nothing really. Forget I said that."

Robert didn't say anything, as he climbed from his car. He waited for Libby to walk round the front. She hadn't answered his question.

She paused at her front door as she searched in her handbag for her keys and then, turning to Robert, indicated that he should follow her inside.

"I need to change out of this ridiculous dress into something more casual. Can I leave you to look around down here? Help yourself to coffee if you like. There's a canister of instant on the worktop in the kitchen, or use the coffee machine."

While Libby ran upstairs, Robert prowled around each room. All the windows were fitted with safety locks and looked to be in good condition. The French windows also had substantial fastenings on them. The only door that looked a bit doubtful was the kitchen one. For some reason there was no extra safety lock, just one of those safety chains that he hated. Robert was testing it against his weight as Libby walked into the kitchen.

"Everything looks okay, except this one. Why is there no safety lock on here – only a chain?" he asked.

"Because it's a new door, and I haven't got round to having one fitted. I thought the chain would be enough. Jem fitted it for me."

"Well, it might be okay, but I'm not sure if someone gave it a really tough shove. If the person was strong and determined, they might be able to pull the screws out. I think we'll get another lock for you. I'll get one next week, and I can fit it if you like. Or if you prefer, a locksmith could do it."

"Robert, you're being very kind. I don't know if I deserve it. Am I a pain?"

He gave her a look. "You probably don't deserve it. And I don't know about a pain, but I do think you're becoming a high-maintenance woman."

Libby stared at him in dismay, until he gave a short laugh. "Libby, I'm teasing! Of course you're not a pain – most of the time anyway. Now, what about that coffee you promised me?"

~~~~~

Later, they sat in the garden while they drank their cappuccinos. Libby was reminded of the last time she had had one down on the front at West Quay. She wondered who his tanned and attractive companion had been that day, and she speculated on how she could bring the subject into their conversation. She was also wildly curious about the child. Supposing Robert was a father? What if he was really married? Surely, Stephanie wouldn't have lied to Libby about Robert needing to find someone, would she?

"Are you sure you haven't got something more pressing to do than play nursemaid to me? What about your boat? Aren't you going sailing today?" she eventually asked.

Robert looked amused. "Libby, my time is my own, and yes, I am planning to spend some time on *Caterina* this weekend. Why?"

"Nothing really."

"I know last time ended badly, and I'm sorry it happened. But are you fishing for an invitation to join me?"

Libby gave a laugh while thinking about it. She missed regular 'messing about in boats', and part of her would have loved an excuse to say 'yes'. Somehow, the thought of Nigel got in the way; thinking of Nigel had her pondering something else. Despite his apparent love of sailing, as far as she knew, Nigel hadn't taken Tourbillon out since the round the island race. Libby wondered why ever not? She knew he was busy, but everyone needed some time away from work.

She gave Robert a smile and shook her head. "No, thank you. I don't want to give Nigel any further cause for complaint. He'll probably get in touch with me later today and explain why he's back home early. Besides, isn't there anyone else you could invite to crew for you?"

"Most of my friends are tied up with their families at the weekend, and Stephanie couldn't manage with her leg in plaster."

"I just wondered about your girlfriend."

Robert frowned. Then his face creased in amusement as he realised who she meant. "Ah! You mean the lovely Diana."

Libby fidgeted as she realised how transparent she had been. "Is that her name?"

"It is."

"When I saw her with you, I thought that I recognised her. Where does she work?"

Putting down his empty coffee cup, Robert glanced at his watch. "I very much doubt that you would have met her unless you've recently paid a visit to Cyprus. Diana lives there now. No, I doubt if she would be able to make it with her baby, unless she left her with Stephanie. She might, I suppose. Anyway, I must be going, thanks for the coffee. You're right. I should take advantage of this good spell of weather and get down to the marina. I think a trip across the Solent to Yarmouth would be nice, or maybe I'll anchor in the Beaulieu River. Last time I was there, I saw an otter swimming across the estuary."

"How lovely! I'd heard they were making a comeback," Libby replied, only half paying attention to his words. So that explained the woman's tan! She lived in Cyprus. When they had first met, Robert had mentioned someone who lived in Cyprus and was connected to him. Wasn't she a cousin or something?

As Robert stood up to leave, Libby suddenly felt downright miserable. For some reason, she didn't want to spend the rest of the day alone. "Will you go on your own then?"

He cast another look at his watch. "I don't suppose so. No, don't get up I'll see myself out. Bye, Libby."

She was left holding the empty coffee cups as Robert walked back into the house. As she heard the door close behind him, she felt even more desolate and couldn't understand why.

Giving herself a scolding, she followed in Robert's footsteps back into the kitchen. She rinsed the cups and popped them in the dishwasher, wondering whether to give Nigel a ring. She was intrigued to discover he was back in Southampton He had been quite emphatic when he had told her he was needed in London. Perhaps the meeting had been cancelled at the last minute. If so, why hadn't he telephoned her?

Libby picked up her mobile and dialled his number. While she waited to be connected, she wandered into her living room. Picking up the television remote control she flicked it on for the local news. Nigel's telephone rang and rang, and while she waited, she watched the latest information concerning the assault on the nurse. With a shock, she heard the description of the attacker; *thin and dark, possibly late thirties to early forties and dressed in a doctor's white coat.* There was some mention that the assailant could have been wearing a wig, so the hair colour wasn't guaranteed. He was wearing a white doctor's coat...surely the attacker wasn't a doctor? Libby was at first horrified to think that a doctor – a man of healing – could be the suspect. Then reason took over. It was, after all, simple to obtain a white lab coat and impersonate any doctor. There were many incidents in history where members of the medical profession turned out to be charlatans and murderers.

Libby was just about to cancel the call to Nigel when it was answered.

"Hello?"

Libby didn't recognise the male voice at the other end and assumed she had misdialled. "I'm sorry, I believe I have a wrong number. Sorry to trouble you." She was about to cancel the call when the voice replied.

"Who are you calling?"

"Nigel St John." She paused. "Is he there?"

There was a pause from the other end, and she thought she caught a brief muffled comment before the voice returned. "No, I'm afraid not. We have this mobile in our possession and want to return it to its owner. Perhaps you could give me more details please? Nigel who and where can I find him?"

Libby had a rapid think. She had no right to give out Nigel's personal details. Her mind whirled as she wondered what she should do. "Er, just where did you find his phone?" she replied. "And who are you?"

Again, there was a slight pause before the voice said, "This is Detective Inspector Collins. The phone was handed in at Southampton General. We've been trying to find the owner so that we can return it."

Chapter 19

Libby was frustrated. Not only had she no means of transport, but now she knew the reason she hadn't been able to get in touch with Nigel. When they'd first met, she thought it strange that Nigel had no landline in his flat. When she had queried it, he explained that he preferred using his mobile. As he was so often away travelling, it was much easier for his patients to contact him that way. That was all very well, but it didn't help her that weekend.

Libby briefly explained to the policeman who Nigel was and her relationship to him. The inspector thanked her for her time and assistance, and after taking her name and number, said they would be in touch if need be. In the meantime, they would hold onto the phone.

Libby wandered around her flat still feeling a bit low. She couldn't decide whether it was because Nigel was here and hadn't bothered getting in touch with her or because she was miffed at Robert, who was probably right now enjoying an exhilarating sail over to the Isle of Wight with the gorgeous Diana by his side, cousin or not.

She decided to give Jem a ring and find out what he and Simon were planning that evening; maybe she could join them somehow.

"Hi Libs, how are you?" Simon answered at once.

"Hi Simon. I'm fine, except I've no car. The blessed thing has finally given up the ghost and conked out on me."

"That's a pity, but I'm not surprised the way you ill-treat it. When will you get it back?"

Libby suppressed a sound of annoyance. Here was someone else lecturing her on how to look after a blessed car. If she had wanted to be an expert on car maintenance, she would have taken an evening class.

"The garage mechanic said sometime on Monday, all being well. I'm on a late duty that day, so hopefully they'll finish fixing it in the morning, and I can pick it up after lunch before I go to work. What are you two doing tonight? I wondered if you'd like to come round and have some supper with me. I know I'm not much of a cook, but I'll do my very best."

"Aw Libby, sorry, we can't. We're halfway to Brighton. We're meeting some old friends for a party and staying overnight. Another time and we'd love to come."

Libby felt even more disconsolate and frustrated at his words. Where were your friends when you needed them most? she thought, after she had said 'goodbye' and wished them a good time. She mooched around the house, tidying a cushion or two and sorting out some old paperbacks to take to the local charity shop. Once she had sorted out a good carrier-bag full, she decided she would take them to the shop now. The walk would do her good, and she had nothing better to do.

The fine warm day was an English summer at its best. The trees lining the road were full and leafy, and Libby thought there was nothing better than the smell of newly-mown grass to set the scene. Walking briskly, she kept turning round and round in her mind thoughts of Nigel and their relationship. During the past few weeks, Libby had tried and tried to recollect when Nigel had proposed to her and given her his ring. It was useless, she just couldn't remember. Neither could she recall making love with him. Surely, if she *really* loved Nigel wouldn't this be the one thing she remembered above all else? This and her feeling of depression were wearing her down. Libby stopped walking and made a snap decision.

It was about time she took hold of her life again and stopped being pathetic! Never could she remember being as feeble-minded as she was right now. The whole thing was absurd. As soon as Nigel contacted her, she was going to tell him it was all over.

She felt like she was living a lie, and Nigel didn't deserve that. Libby had meant it when she had said she would wear his ring again when she recovered her memory, but somehow she had this feeling she and Nigel were never meant to be. Now that her mind was made up, she felt a weight lifting from her heart. She knew he would be annoyed and upset, but she truly believed this was the right thing to do. With a lighter and almost joyous tread to her step, she turned towards home.

Chapter 20

The watcher had bungled last night. For the first time, a mistake had been made and that was *nothing* like usual. The stupid woman had surprisingly put up quite a fight. Normally the victim was caught unawares and terrified when they saw the scalpel blade in front of their throat. The watcher thought the choice had been a good one this time. She was the right age, colouring and height, and a nurse. Every move of hers had been followed during the past week, and the watcher thought she would be ideal as a victim before the *final one*. The watcher had felt the urge the day before and decided to chance a hand one more time. It felt so good to once again emerge from watcher to *attacker*. Dressed in dark clothes, complete with wig and stage make-up, it was so simple to don the doctor's white coat and mingle with the hospital visitors and staff. Security was nowhere near as good as it could be, and it was easy to engage the woman in flattering conversation while sharing a cigarette with her.

That part of the hospital, the teaching part, was usually quiet, and the west wing was completely deserted at that time of night. The shadows cast from the red-brick walls were long and dark, making it the perfect setting. The nurse was so relaxed when asked for her telephone number, and it was easy to approach her from behind as she wrote it down on a scrap of paper. Oh, the ecstasy as the look on her face turned to one of terror! When she understood and realised her mistake too late, the faithful blade began its glorious work.

The attacker was furious when she dodged the next cut to her face. She recovered her poise enough by kicking out viciously against the attackers' shin and then recoiled before jabbing at the attacker's face with her pen. Despite her desperate attempt to escape, there was a blissful moment when the scalpel sliced through her flesh before she managed to slip from her attacker's grasp and run screaming towards the main building.

The attacker knew of a shortcut leading onto a back road which would eventually come to the university buildings. The attacker had left a car there, concealed in the shadows, and it was an easy task to remove the coat and wig and roll them up into a ball while moving towards the getaway. All that was left to do now was go home, take a shower and change clothes. An alibi would be good too. There were a couple of parties that night that were bound to be crowded, boozy affairs. No one would even notice someone arriving late. It was simple to slip in the back way, take a glass of wine and act like they had been there for hours. It was simple for someone with such excellent acting capabilities.

Chapter 21

It was a draught on her neck that woke her. After her hangover and short night before, Libby knew she needed an early one. She cooked a simple meal for herself and, feeling the need for some company, ate it in front of the television. Being summer, there was little stimulating drama to become involved in, and after watching half an hour of drivel, she decided it was time for bed. An hour reading a good book with a cup of cocoa would be heaven after a soothing and relaxing hot bath to settle her nerves.

Feeling self-indulgent, Libby added a capful of her precious *Jo Malone* lime, basil and mandarin bath oil and sank down in the silky warm water. Allowing her mind to wander, she lay back and dozed, blissfully lulled by the scent of the oil and candles. She dreamed she was floating in the Caribbean Sea, a warm sun gently kissing her skin…a soft caressing breeze blowing down upon…

…Libby's eyes flew open. She wasn't floating, nor was she lying in the sun, but she did feel a cool draught on her skin. Troubled, she sat up and listened. Maybe Rommie, her cat, had just entered by her cat-flap creating a draught.

Straining her ears, she thought she heard a soft footfall on the tiled floor in the kitchen. With trembling fingers, she whisked her bath towel from the stool next to her tub and slowly stood up. The cooling water ran down her stomach and thighs as she wrapped the towel around her. Her heart was thudding in her breast as she moved stealthily from the water onto the floor, ensuring she didn't make a sound. *There it was again*! A definite noise came from the direction of her kitchen. Feeling vulnerable, she looked around in terror. If only there was something to protect herself with in here.

In vain, she cast her eye over the pile of fresh towels and bottles of shampoo and creams. She didn't possess as much as a wooden loofah! Quivering with fright, she crossed over to the door. There was a key in the lock which she rarely used because it was stiff and unyielding. She prayed to God she could turn it. As she turned the key, there was a definite 'click' that, to her ears, sounded like a crack from a pistol. Apart from the locked door, she was completely defenceless.

Feeling exposed in her nudity, Libby grabbed her bathrobe and pulled it on, knotting the belt tightly round her waist. There was a window in the room, but she doubted whether she could climb through it, as it looked too small even for her slight frame. If she stood on the stool, she could open the window wider and could scream for help – but would anyone hear her despite the room being in the front of the flat? Would it just let the intruder know she was there? Uncertain as what to do, Libby felt something hard in her robe pocket, and putting her hand inside, discovered her mobile phone.

She could hardly grip the telephone as her hands were shaking so much, and just as she pressed the first emergency number nine digit, she heard the closing of the front door and footsteps moving swiftly away down the path. At first, Libby felt overwhelming relief. With tears threatening to spill down her cheeks she slumped onto the bathroom floor. Recovering her composure, she discovered she was shaking once more. This time, it was nothing to do with her fear. As resolve flooded into her body, she was aware of how furious she was. Who had been in her flat, her home? How did they manage to get in?

Convinced whoever it was had long gone, Libby unlocked the bathroom door, grabbed a heavy vase from the hall table and walked towards her kitchen. Apart from a slight tangy, almost citrus scent lingering in the still air, the room was empty, as was her living room and small study. What was more, not only had the prowler left, but there was no evidence of a break-in. Her kitchen door and all the windows were locked, and the safety chain was still in place. Her front door was of course closed, and entry could only be obtained by the Yale lock key. As Libby wandered round each room again, checking cupboards, doors and windows, a chill settled in her stomach.

If everything was as it should be – there were no faulty catches, or broken windows – then the intruder must have let himself in with a *duplicate key*.

Chapter 22

"I know I've been in hospital recently, and some things have remained muzzy since being knocked out, but I swear there was someone in my flat."

The two policemen exchanged looks at her choice of words. The senior officer made a slight movement with his head to indicate he was going outside, and the other continued. "Now, Miss Hunter, if in future you think you might have a burglar or any further scares, please don't hesitate to get in touch with us. We can have a car outside your place within minutes. I'll make sure a patrol car passes this way during the night too, just to keep an eye on the area. Remember, we're just a phone call away."

Libby didn't know whether to feel relieved or scared witless. She knew the younger police constable, as he lived just round the corner and visited the local pub when off duty. As soon as they had arrived, she recognised his square features and squat body. Weighing in at about 190 pounds, she doubted whether anyone would mess with him!

She got the distinct impression the police officers didn't believe her when she told them her story about hearing someone prowling around in her kitchen and watched their faces while they checked her windows and doors. Of course, they didn't think she was making it all up, only that they thought she had imagined it. Both men were very polite and patient and seemed quite nice about it, but Libby guessed they weren't going to give it much more thought, especially after informing them that no one else had a key to her home and that there was no apparent sign of a break-in.

"Righto then, we'll be on our way. I'd get a bolt fitted to the front door, if I were you, and maybe another on the kitchen door. Pop into the station tomorrow morning, and you can sign your statement. Goodnight."

Libby saw him out and watched as he joined his colleague in the patrol car. After a brief wave, she was on her own once again. Shutting the door behind them, she leaned against it, confused, fed up and annoyed. Had she heard footsteps? She was sure she hadn't imagined it, and she wasn't going round the bend yet! She flicked the dead bolt on the Yale and wandered back into her kitchen. When in doubt, have a cup of tea, she thought.

Waiting for the kettle to boil, she wondered if by some chance someone did have a duplicate key in their possession. The locksmith company? Certainly none of her friends. What was the chance of someone having a whole bunch of Yale keys with one that fitted her lock? She had bought the flat about a year ago from an estate agent who seemed perfectly respectable. They displayed all the right credentials, and the man who had conducted the sale was the owner-manager, so the chances of a duplicate key emanating from there were slim. There must be another explanation she decided.

Every idea she came up with seemed doubtful. It was more likely she had forgotten to flick the lock in place, and someone had slid a credit card up the crack between the door and the frame, tripping the lock. She felt sure she had seen it done in a crime serial on television some time ago.

A soft meow had Libby turning towards the back door, and she found her cat shivering outside. Libby bent down and picked her up in her arms. "What's the matter, little one?" she said, stroking her soft fur. As she lifted her hand away from the cat she realised her hand was covered in blood, and the cat meowed pitifully once more. On closer inspection, Libby discovered a large cut along the side on the animal's flank. Not a deep incision, but enough to ensure plenty of free-flowing blood. In alarm, Libby grabbed her first aid box and cleaned the wound which luckily soon stopped bleeding. She wondered how it had happened and what the cat had caught herself on to cause the wound. When she had finished, Libby placed Rommie in her basket and stood back watching her. For a moment, it crossed her mind that maybe someone had actually inflicted the wound, and the idea made her feel quite sick. Don't go there, she thought. The cat often came in scratched after a fracas with next door's tom. Surely nobody would be so horrible to hurt an innocent animal?

Taking her tea with her, she went to her bedroom and settled herself in bed. She doubted whether she would get to sleep. It had been the strangest of days. It had started when she woke up in Robert's guest bedroom, then she saw Nigel as he sped past in his car, had coffee with Robert in her garden and now this latest odd and scary episode, ending with her injured cat. She didn't care what the policemen thought. She *knew* someone had entered her house uninvited and bolted when they realised the flat wasn't unoccupied.

Someone had wanted to get into her home when it was empty. Libby had two questions. Who and why?

Chapter 23

Back at work, Libby found tightened security at the hospital and especially around the houses shared by nurses. More CCTV cameras were being installed, and there appeared to be an extra security staff presence in the grounds. Everyone was on tenterhooks and the female nurses were making sure no one walked alone when they arrived or left the hospital during the dark hours. Once inside the building, the staff were more relaxed, with business going on much as normal, despite the rumours.

Libby already had the up-to-date information from Jem, who was now back from his weekend in Brighton, and Lisa was willing to fill her in on any detail he had missed out.

"We've already had staff crying off night duty. At the moment, we're two down for tonight and possibly tomorrow, and they can't all be legitimately sick. '*Human Remains*' are at their wit's end recruiting more agency staff and it's getting ridiculous. So far, I've managed not to get us involved, because I know you loathe night duty, but who knows, if this happens again?" Lisa said, while handing her early day report over to Libby. "I hear your car finally gave up the ghost on Saturday. Have you got it back yet?"

"Yes. It's all fixed and the garage says it's not in bad nick considering how badly I treat it. Apparently, it should have had a service eighteen months ago. I suppose time just flew, and I forgot."

"What was the matter with it then?"

"Um, quite a list of things apparently. I've had to pay out for a new battery, plugs, something to do with the carburettor and two new tyres. It's cost me a packet, despite Robert telling me they were reasonable."

"Well, they might well be, and quite honestly you deserve to pay. Honestly Libby, you should have had it done ages ago. I have mine serviced regular as clockwork."

"That's because you've got a fantastic husband who takes care of things like that for you. You know how he adores you. You'll never have to worry."

Lisa gave her a look which could only be described as self-satisfied and smug. She grinned and nodded. "And pretty soon he's going to be doing a lot more."

Libby shot her a look. "Do you mean what I think you mean?" she asked, her eyes big and round in excitement.

Lisa giggled. "Yes!"

"Oh, congratulations! When it's due? Have you had a scan yet? Do you know what it is?"

Lisa laughed. "Whoa! Slow down please! First, I'm only about seven weeks and no I've not had a scan, and of course I don't know what I'm having. Give me time!"

Libby went over and gave her a hug. "I am so pleased for you, and I have to admit I am a little jealous. I know I'd love a baby some time when I finally meet the right man."

Lisa's look was gentle as she gazed at her friend. "Does this mean you and Nigel aren't—?"

Libby gave a sigh and shook her head. "I haven't said anything to him yet. I only made my mind up over the weekend. No one else knows, not that many knew we were seeing each other anyway." She looked and sounded miserable.

It was Lisa's turn to give her a hug. "I am sorry it hasn't worked out. Can I ask why or is it too private?"

Libby thought over her words. "If you don't mind, I don't want to talk about it yet, at least not until I've spoken to Nigel. There are one or two things I want to have out with him, and I don't think it's fair to tell you before him. I promise I'll let you know as soon as I can."

"Of course, you must speak to him first. I'm sure you owe him that. All I'll say at this stage is that I'm not really surprised. You didn't come over as 'blushing bride' material. Perhaps it's for the best."

"Perhaps," Libby echoed her despondently.

"I'm sure the right man is waiting for you somewhere. You just have to find that somewhere," she said, giving her a friendly squeeze on the arm.

Libby nodded looking unconvinced. "I'm beginning to believe I'm hopeless when it comes to finding the right man. But that may be the least of my worries."

"Why? What's happened now?"

Libby exhaled loudly. "I'm sure I had an intruder over the weekend."

Lisa covered her mouth with her hand in horror. "Oh my God! That's awful! Tell me what happened."

Libby went over the events of that night, missing nothing out, even down to her suspicion that she believed the police thought she had an over-fertile imagination.

"The strange thing is there was absolutely no sign of any break-in. Not a window broken or a door left open, nothing. And finally, Rommie turned up injured. For one awful moment, I did wonder if it was anything to do with the intruder, but I can't be sure."

"It's downright curious and spooky, and perfectly horrid for you." Lisa looked suitably shocked.

"I can only think I forgot to deadlock the Yale on my front door, and somehow, someone managed to trip the lock and get in. The window safety catches are all new and perfectly secure. I had Robert check them earlier that weekend."

"Robert? Oh, I remember, the helicopter rescue pilot. What was he doing there, you dark horse? And why would he check the locks for you?"

Libby sighed and flashed Lisa a guilty look. "It's a long story, and I'll tell you about it some other time. All you need to know is that I'd told him only that day I'd been having some odd feelings of being watched. He was so nice and a perfect gentleman. While I was getting changed, he checked the doors and windows over for me."

Lisa didn't say anything immediately, but looked a bit sceptical over Libby's explanation for a few seconds. "So while you were upstairs changing your clothes, you left a relative stranger in your house, touching your windows and doors! What if he'd 'accidently' left one open? Libby, how well do you know this man?'

Libby looked uncomfortable and replied. "Fairly well. No nothing like that! We're just good friends, and I don't believe he'd have done anything so stupid. He was very thorough in checking the place over and even suggested another lock for the back door."

"Okay, but I'm just saying you don't really know him. He's only been around for a few weeks. What about keys? Has anyone got a spare one, like a neighbour as an emergency, or do you keep one hidden in the garden?"

"No. No one has a spare."

"Have you lent one to anyone recently? And you do realise it's very easy to take an imprint of a key in a lump of children's plasticine don't you?"

There was a short silence while Libby thought. When Lisa saw her cheeks go pink, she knew she was right.

"Well? You have, haven't you?"

"The only person who has had ready access to my keys is Nigel when I was in hospital. I lent them to him when he came over to get some of my clothes and toiletries."

Lisa expelled her breath noisily. "I see. And, of course, Robert could have taken an imprint."

"Lisa, you have a terrible mind! Both of these men are friends and one I'm supposed to be engaged to! I'm sure neither would do anything to frighten me. Why would they?"

"Libby, call me an interfering old busybody if you like, but right at this minute with all that's been going on around here *and* with nurses, I don't trust anyone! You're an attractive woman, single, you live alone, and you're a *nurse*! You say you've been experiencing some odd feelings about being watched, and yet you're so silly, letting strange men into your house. Honestly!"

"Okay, okay. I get the message." She held her hands out in front of her friend demonstrating her understanding. "You're right. Maybe I have been foolish and too trustworthy. I'll get the locks looked at by a locksmith and have extra bolts fitted. If it makes you happier, I'll change the front and back door locks too. I don't know when I can do it, but I'll ring someone this afternoon."

"Good! I'm pleased, and I'm going to check that you do, even if I have to get my own man to do it for you. What's more, in case you haven't already told Jem, I'm going to do it for you. If there's anyone you can trust it's him and Simon. Jem will certainly keep an eye on you. Right now, let's get moving. We have a ward to run and at least four more theatre cases to get ready for this afternoon. The first two have had their pre-meds and the other two – here are their notes – are due in about half an hour," she said, casting a quick glance at her fob watch and passed the patients' papers to Libby. "I have just about time to pay a quick visit to another ward. If you can hold the fort here for me, I'll only be about ten minutes."

Before Libby could answer, Lisa had already left the office. Libby stared at the bundle of notes in her hands, not really seeing them. If she knew Lisa as well as she thought she did, then Libby knew full well where she had dashed off to. It didn't take a lot of imagination to guess Lisa was enlightening Jem about Libby's so-called foolishness. She didn't know whether to be pleased or miffed at her friend's good intentions.

~~~~~

The afternoon proved to be manic. As well as the theatre list, there was a major road traffic accident and all free beds on the surgical wards were soon occupied with the victims. As fast as Libby sorted her theatre patients, the bed manager was breathing down her neck for her to free up more beds for the accident cases that were still being brought in. Libby couldn't remember a day like it and really couldn't see herself getting off at nine o'clock that evening – there was just too much to do, especially with so many staff calling in 'sick'.

As nine o'clock approached, she decided she might just as well stay here for another hour or so and give the beleaguered night staff a hand before she went off duty. She had nothing to go home for anyway, and she still hadn't managed to get in touch with Nigel, who apparently was up in London once again. He was proving to be as enigmatic and elusive as the Scarlet Pimpernel she thought. She couldn't even tell him about her intruder! This was becoming ludicrous.

Libby was in two minds about telling Nigel what she had decided over the weekend. She felt sure he would fly off the deep end in a temper, and she wasn't sure how she would handle him in her exhausted state. She also wanted to tell him face to face. Despite feeling more and more annoyed with him each hour he failed to get in touch with her, she felt she owed him that much. They were meant to be engaged, after all.

The late day workers were beginning to depart as the night shift gradually took over. Just before midnight, Libby decided she had had enough, and things were finally settling down. Thankfully, her ward was now fully covered, and she wasn't required to work through the night, which she would have loathed. After handing over to a senior staff nurse, Libby changed out of her grubby uniform into her own casual clothes. After wearily dragging a comb through her hair, she was about to leave when her mobile telephone rang. Resisting a sigh, she glanced at the LCD screen and realised she didn't recognise the number, nor could she imagine who would be calling her at that time of night.

"Libby? Where are you?"

"Nigel! I could ask you the same question," she said, irritation clearly evident in her voice. "Where the devil are you? I've been trying to get hold of you all day. Your secretary was useless and so tight-lipped, I couldn't get any information out of her. You have no idea what I've been through the last few—"

"Darling, I'm still in London. I lost my telephone and didn't realise it until late in the evening. I couldn't arrange another one as it was too late in the day."

"I know all that."

"You know?"

"Yes. I rang you some time over the weekend, and the police answered my call to your phone. Apparently, they found it."

"Ah. Ah yes, of course. When was this?"

Libby thought. She couldn't really remember because so much had happened during the last three days, she was now almost reeling with fatigue. If only he would listen.

"Sorry, Nigel, I can't recall off hand, I'm so tired. You've heard what's happened here today, I expect?"

"Yes. We saw it on the television news. Terrible business"

"Why are you still up there? Why didn't you get in touch sooner? You could have borrowed a phone surely?" She felt like screaming at his lack of understanding. *We?* What was going on?

"Well actually, I was involved in a bit of an accident myself."

Instantly, Libby felt alarm run through her. "Oh no! What's happened? Are you hurt?" How could she have been so awful? She had just given him a real grilling concerning his whereabouts and whinging about why he hadn't contacted her, and all the time he had been in an accident.

"Nothing serious. Don't worry your pretty little head. I was careless. I slipped and fell and injured my leg. Just some bruising and a few cuts. It's a little difficult to drive at the moment, but I'll be home in a day or so. I'm quite comfortable staying in the London house. Besides, you won't know this, but Stella, my ex-wife, is here with me. She's used to me of old and is quite happy to lend a hand while I recover."

"Oh Nigel, and here I am behaving like a fishwife. I'm so sorry, but I'm glad you're not badly injured. Can you walk okay? If not, at least I can ferry you around." *So his ex-wife was part of the 'we'.*

"Oh yes. I just told you, I'm just bruised. It'll heal pretty quickly, and Stella can drive me if needed. Libby, I've been thinking—"

"Yes?"

"About you moving in with me." Libby listened as he continued. "I think, in view of what you said last week, we need to take things slowly, give ourselves time to think and a bit of breathing space. Just for a short while, if that's all right with you; about a couple of weeks?"

Libby could hardly stop herself from breathing a sigh of relief. At least she wasn't going to have to tell him immediately what she thought her true feelings were. She could work up to it gently.

"I understand. That's fine with me, Nigel. We'll wait. All you need to do is get fit again."

Surprisingly, Nigel ignored what Libby had said and asked her what she had told the police about him.

"Nothing much. I just told them who you were and our relationship. Was that okay? I didn't divulge anything private about you. Why?"

"Oh nothing. That's fine, Libby. I was just checking."

"Where did they find your mobile anyway?"

"Oh, somewhere around the hospital grounds. I must have lost it before I left for London. It doesn't matter because I have this as a replacement until I get back to Southampton. Make a note of this number will you, in case you need to ring me?"

"Of course."

Nigel said 'goodbye' and Libby ended the call. She still hadn't managed to tell him about her intruder. How unfortunate he should have met with an accident, she thought. Libby knew how livid being immobile would make Nigel, and yet again how fortuitous it was his ex-wife was on the scene to keep an eye on him. Libby would have liked to ask about Stella. She was curious about Nigel's former wife. She wondered how long she would be over from America and whether they often met up in town during her visits. Libby knew about the London house in Knightsbridge and idly speculated on just who owned it. Nigel had told Libby he and Stella were divorced, but he had never said who retained which of their various houses. Libby presumed

Nigel owned his penthouse apartment in Southampton because he had moved there after the split. Again, she pondered whether Stella ever stayed with Nigel there. It was unlikely; Nigel had never mentioned it, and when Libby had first been shown round the place, she hadn't noticed any items belonging to a female visitor, guest or otherwise.

Chapter 24

After finishing his call to Libby, Nigel replaced his mobile in his trouser pocket and poured himself a last glass of Rioja before calling it a night. He looked pensive as he carefully went over what he and Libby had been discussing. He had seen the dreadful accident on the Southampton area motorway on the televised evening news, and he could well imagine the carnage caused in the twelve vehicle pile-up. Libby had sounded quite drained and almost tearful as she took his call. While he was pouring the wine, Stella limped into the kitchen, perched herself onto one of the bar stools and propped a bandaged leg up onto an adjacent one.

"Like another?" he asked, indicating the bottle and noting enough wine for one more glass.

"Better not. I've just taken another couple of painkillers and they might not agree with each other. Besides it's getting late. Why are you still drinking, Nigel? You don't usually have as much."

He shrugged. "It's been a long day, and I felt like one. I've just spoken to Libby."

Stella smiled. "Was she all right? Did you tell her?"

Nigel looked at Stella thoughtfully before immediately replying. "She was fine, just sounded very tired and strung up."

She nodded. "I'm not surprised. Dealing with a major accident is usually ghastly, especially if you're on a surgical ward as you have to deal with patients' wounds *and* their mental anguish. What I really meant was, did you tell her about us?"

"Yes. But in a roundabout way."

Stella frowned and looked annoyed, so he explained. "I didn't say it was you who'd had an accident. I said it was me, and you happened to be here in London, and very conveniently, you are able to take care of me."

"Nigel, you never change do you? You really are a coward at times. You never said a word, did you?"

"Maybe it's for the best, Stella. Why should I hurt her unnecessarily?"

Stella gave a short almost bitter laugh. "Nigel, you never care about the pain you cause. You must have had dozens of women over the years, and not once has it meant anything to you, except for adding another notch to your bedpost, so why would you start now?"

"Stella, please darling. We've both had a long day after a long weekend. I don't want to quarrel with you."

Stella looked immediately contrite. She edged down off her stool and put her arms around him. "I'm sure you know what you're doing, sweetheart. Anyway, don't let's talk about her anymore. Let's talk about us; that's so much more interesting. I want to know what you're planning for our future. Perhaps I will chance another glass of wine after all." A look of mischief mixed with anticipation flitted across her features.

Nigel gathered Stella into his arms and gazed into her face. Her body was slim and lightly tanned, and as he drew her closer to him, he realised how well-muscled she was these days. Stella was a recent member of some gym or other, and her newfound keenness was evidently paying off. As her hand brushed against his groin, he recognised the old familiar ritual of seduction.

~~~~~

While Stella slept, Nigel was restless as he wrestled with his conscience. Moving slowly so as not to wake her, he slipped from under the covers and padded barefoot into the kitchen, not bothering to switch on a light. Stella had always been an excellent partner in bed, and tonight her appetite almost matched his own; not quite, but there was something almost feral in her lovemaking. Sex with her nowadays was quite exceptional, and Nigel wondered why. She was evidently looking after herself – her body was lean and hard

– but in the past, sex hadn't figured quite the same with her as it did him.

Then there was Libby. Nigel hadn't wanted to forestall his plans for Libby moving in with him, but with Stella showing up a few days ago and clearly indicating she was intending to stay with him when he went back down to Southampton, he knew there was no other option. What he didn't understand was how Stella had found out about Libby in the first place. It wasn't any of her business, but deep down, Nigel recognised that Stella finding out about his latest love was always on the cards. During their time together, Stella managed to develop an uncanny awareness of when Nigel was cheating on her. When they were first married, Nigel was able to conduct his extra-marital affairs easily without Stella's knowledge. It wasn't until he accidently made one of his lovers pregnant that she guessed where he was spending a major part of his spare time, and since then, she had made it her business. Being a gynaecologist, Nigel knew exactly what to do with an unwanted pregnancy, but once Stella found out, he soon realised she was having no more of his philandering – unless, of course, he was clever enough to carry on without her knowing.

Looking back on those years, Nigel supposed Stella still retained that mysterious perception, even now when she was far away in New York or London. How else would she have known about Libby, unless she had someone spying on him? Nigel gave a sigh. He still loved Stella in his own way. She possessed this hold over him, but she was too complicated and erratic to live with full-time. She also knew far too much about him and some of his odd little ways. Libby was somewhat simpler and less demanding, more malleable.

This time, though, he thought his planning was going well. None of their joint friends knew about their relationship, and Libby losing her memory had been an added bonus. It still was, as she hadn't twigged they'd never been engaged and Nigel was anxious she never would, until it was too late.

It was annoying she was being a stickler over wearing her engagement ring, but he was sure she would eventually give in and wear it with pride. He only needed patience, and Nigel had plenty of that.

Chapter 25

The watcher picked up the briefcase, and after twiddling the security lock until the right combination showed, flicked open the catches. Tucked inside behind one of the leather dividers, the watcher withdrew a slim jeweller's box and opened it. Nestling on the black velvet was an exquisite ankle bracelet made of heavy silver. The stalker fingered the smooth worked metal with a tender touch and then turned the bracelet over. On the inside were the words that had been inscribed earlier, "*Mine, all mine.*"

Each one had been given such a bracelet, and they had worn it with pride, not knowing that the gift singled them out. It was as befitting as a gift could be. *They* were the chosen ones.

The stalker gave a smile and lovingly replaced the bracelet in the box. It was almost time. Soon, very soon, the final one would receive her gift.

Chapter 26

'The woman injured in the attack last night, a 31-year-old staff nurse, was detained in St Thomas's Hospital in London. She is being kept in the intensive care unit while the medical staff come to a decision regarding her surgery. The woman was on night shift duty when she was savagely attacked. The only information police have released at this stage is that she suffered severe lacerations to her face and abdomen. The weapon has not been identified. She remains stable. Any possible witnesses to this deplorable attack should contact....'

Robert switched the television off as Diana entered the living room. She looked at Robert. "What? Why did you turn it off? I don't mind you watching TV, you know. Please don't feel you have to entertain me." She sat down in an easy chair and eased the baby from her shoulder. "Poppy's hungry early today. I'm waiting for her bottle to warm. She's already scoffed her solids."

Robert smiled at the gappy-toothed infant as she cooed at him from her mother's lap. "Would you like to give it to her? She's very obliging."

Robert looked very unsure as Diana handed him a square of muslin, indicating it was 'just in case she's sick' and to protect his clothes. "Er, I'm not too sure about this, Di." He squirmed in his chair.

Diana laughed as she walked back towards the kitchen. "Don't be such a coward. She won't bite you know. Steve's become a real dab hand at feeding her." Robert jiggled the baby around a bit, obviously scared witless she just might start crying if she was separated from her mother.

"Here you are. Are you comfortable? That's it. Just lean back in your chair and relax! She knows what to do," Diana said, holding a warmed bottle of milk out to Robert. "I believe she's grown in the short time we've been here, Steve's going to notice a difference with his darling daughter when he arrives from Cyprus."

"It's all right for Steve – he's had practice recently. It's been ages since I've done this."

Diana studied him while he fed her baby. She thought she knew what was going through his mind. She decided to say nothing, thinking the contact with an infant would do him good. Eight ounces of milk later, a burped, contented Poppy was happily playing with her assortment of rattles once Diana relieved Robert of his nursing duties.

"That wasn't too bad, was it?" she asked gently.

Robert glanced at her, and Diana knew instantly he understood she hadn't simply meant feeding her child. "Do you want to talk? I loved her too you know."

~~~~~

Robert sighed. Diana was right. Of all the people he knew, his cousin, Diana, had been the closest to his dead wife, Morwenna. In fact it had been her who had introduced the dark-haired, elven-faced Welsh girl to the young Royal Air Force pilot all those years ago. Robert knew Diana had noticed how he and her best friend became tongue-tied in each other's presence. She had noticed the surreptitious looks and sidelong glances that eventually led to a then bashful Robert asking the bright, pretty nurse out to the pictures.

After that initial painful phase of discovering and overcoming their shyness, within weeks, Robert and Morwenna were head over heels in love. Robert knew he was up for promotion leading to an overseas posting, so forestalling his seniors at work, he asked Morwenna to be his wife.

Even now, he still recalled the look of happiness and astonishment on his darling girl's face when he had knelt down on one knee and produced a sapphire – her birthstone – engagement ring. "Please say 'yes'," he had begged from his place on the ground, gazing into her eyes with an intensity she found compelling. "If you refuse me, I don't know what I'll do."

In response, she had flung her arms around him and whispered a breathy answer in his ear. When they returned home together, it was Diana to whom they gave their exciting news.

"I knew it," she said, laughing. "As soon as I saw you two together, I reckoned you would hit it off. Mind you, even I'm a bit surprised at how quickly you've made your decision. Has this got anything to do with your pending promotion, Robert? Wait until Stephanie hears about this! She's been like the proverbial cat on a hot tin roof ever since I told her about you. I can hardly wait to see her face."

At first, Robert had been appalled that his well-meaning but ever-meddling cousin, Diana, had obviously been discussing him and Morwenna with his sister. He had rolled his eyes in dismay at Morwenna, who had simply giggled at his discomfiture and showed an admiring Diana her sparkling ring.

Stephanie and Diana decided to take things in hand and, between them, assisted Morwenna towards organising a simple, but tasteful wedding. Over the years since his wife's death, the memory of her standing in her wedding dress, slender and beautiful before him, still sent a shaft of remorse through him.

Robert and Morwenna enjoyed seven years together. Morwenna loved accompanying her handsome husband on some of his overseas tours and revelled in exploring far-eastern exotic countries. They lived well and it was obvious to all their friends that they had the perfect marriage. It was during Robert's posting back in England that Morwenna discovered she was expecting their first baby. Both parents were thrilled when their tiny daughter arrived during a cold and blustery December, and after listening to the maternity ward nurses singing Christmas carols as they went about their duties, Morwenna would hear of no other name for her baby girl. A few weeks later, she was christened Carole.

Fatherhood took Robert by surprise, and he often found himself hovering round his daughter's cot much to Morwenna's amusement. He considered those days to be among the best of his life.

He and Morwenna spent much of their free time discovering the English countryside. A favourite place of theirs was situated on the South Downs and coast, the Seven Sisters Country Park. This area comprised 280 hectares of chalk cliffs, meandering river valley and open chalk grassland. It was an immensely popular place for outdoor activities including walking, bird watching, cycling and canoeing.

"Let's take a picnic to the Seven Sisters Park this afternoon," Robert said, as he wandered into the kitchen of their home. "The weather's been lousy for the past couple of weeks, and it would be good to get some fresh air in our lungs."

Morwenna looked doubtful as she glanced out of the window. "Are you sure? It's a fair journey, and although it's stopped raining, it's still grey and dull outside."

"Come on, sweetheart, where's your spirit? A little rain never hurt anybody. We can throw the raincoats in the back of the car, and we can be there in less than two hours. Besides, I want to try out the new camera you bought me. I've hardly used it since Christmas."

Morwenna had laughed at his enthusiasm and began searching through her fridge and cupboards for the makings of a tasty picnic. "You know we'll probably end up eating everything in the car, don't you?"

Robert leant over his daughter's buggy with a smile. "We think Mummy's being a bit of a wet blanket, don't we? We'll have to change her mind." Carole giggled and cooed kicking the soft cotton blanket from her legs in excitement. "Look, Morwenna, Carole wants to go!"

The drive was uneventful. With light traffic on the roads they made good time. The rain held off, and the sun even peeped from behind a bank of clouds as the little family strolled along the cliff top with baby Carole snugly nestled in a baby carrier on Robert's back. When a chill wind and mist began to roll in from the sea, Robert decided it was time to head back to the car and enjoy some hot soup and filled crusty rolls. They had parked the car on the top of the cliffs about fifty yards away from the edge and just off the track, where they could sit watching the spume-topped waves roll in.

"It was good idea of yours to get out," Morwenna agreed, once they were back in the car. "I'll feed baby, and then with luck, she'll sleep on the way home." She settled down to nurse Carole.

"Okay, while you're busy, I'll take myself off along the cliff top the other way and take some more photographs. I might be able to get some good shots with this light. It's almost eerie with the weak sun and the sea mist rolling in. I'll be gone about fifteen minutes if that's all right? Keep the car doors locked while I'm gone, will you?"

Morwenna agreed it was a good idea, and Robert gave her a loving kiss before leaving the car. The cliff top path ran along the edge. It was well worn and obviously a favourite with walkers, judging by the eroded edges and the width of it. Robert knew just the right spot to take his photographs. There was a part of the cliff which showed exposed fossils. With the sun sinking fast in the west, Robert thought he could get a perfect composition. The area was slightly further than he thought, and despite the rain holding off that day, there were deep puddles dotted here and there. He found the area he had been looking for and was disappointed to find there had been a recent rock fall. Where the cliff had sloped before with a natural grace and beauty, now there was a gaping hole. Disappointed, he began the muddy wet walk back to the car, looking forward to another cup of hot tea.

He hadn't gone more than a few yards, when there was a slight tremor at his feet and he heard a rumbling in the distance. A slight crack appeared in the turf where his feet were, and he moved away from the cliff edge with alarm. The whole area was soggy with the recent rain. Robert suddenly felt a pang of worry shoot through him. *He had left his wife and baby in the car not that far from the cliff's edge.*

Robert began to run.

When he reached the area where he had left Morwenna and the baby, there was nothing to be seen. It was empty. Moreover the spot wasn't just empty, there was *nothing there.* There was a gaping hole now where the car and its occupants had been sited near the edge of the cliff. About eighty feet along the cliff edge, the turf was ragged and torn with exposed white chalk and stone.

~~~~~

There had been an inquest, and for some time, Robert had been described by lesser newspapers as 'that infamous pilot who left his family to fall to their deaths at one of England's most famous beauty spots'. Robert did nothing to dispel the nasty rumours about deliberately parking his car at a remote spot during a time of serious risk of cliff erosion, even when one of the reporters hounding him was quite scandalous with her accusations. Instead, Robert was set on cutting himself off from friends and family, believing he could deal with the rumours and his own guilt by himself.

Even his sister and cousin found it difficult to break through his hard shell to help him with his grief.

It took Robert many years to come to terms with his supposed irresponsibility. During that time, despite meeting other women on a casual basis, he never found another that came near to, let alone replace, his Morwenna. Since the onslaught of the horrendous allegations from the female reporter, for the first time in his life, he lost his respect for mankind, especially women.

Chapter 27

The latest idea had been so easy! The success rate so far had been almost 100 per cent. Only once had the watcher failed to leave a mark, a warning of what was to come. Mistakes were *not* an option. Never mind, things were well on their way now. Just a few days to settle down and get with the flow…and then it would be all over. The watcher would have accomplished all that was set out to be done.

The latest women had all been tasters… hors d'oeuvres, if you like…the watcher had never meant to *kill* any of them…that fate was reserved for Libby.

Too bad there was an increase in security, but no matter, the watcher *knew* how to get in, knew how to perform the last episode. Everything had been handed on a plate, and without knowing it, the victim had unwittingly agreed.

Chapter 28

Libby wasn't anticipating Robert's call that evening. When she returned home from work, she had been grateful to slip out of her work clothes. She took a cooling shower and looked forward to an evening of leisure. She had felt almost light-hearted ever since her last telephone call with Nigel when he asked for a delay in her moving in with him. Libby wasn't sure, but she guessed it was something to do with the previous Mrs St John. Perhaps things were changing between them. They could even be getting back together again for all she knew.

Libby paused as she decided what she was going to cook for supper. She eyed a couple of chicken breasts in the refrigerator and thought she might try her hand at Green Thai Curry. She had a new recipe book and most of the ingredients. The method didn't look particularly difficult.

She checked through her kitchen cupboard and selected everything she needed to make the green curry paste. What was perhaps most surprising was her reaction to Nigel's postponement. She was feeling almost a little guilty as a result of his proposal. She scolded herself. *For goodness sake, woman!* He is offering you a chance to think things over. True, she had already decided a few days ago she wanted to split up, because she knew things were not right between them, but she still believed she was the guilty party. Nigel just wanted them to be together; she was the one who was shilly-shallying. She knew, when it finally came down to it, she was going to tell him 'no'. She didn't want to marry him, but that was a strange thing too. She couldn't actually remember Nigel mentioning marriage. Oh yes, he had talked about their moving in together and sharing a life, but marriage was never mentioned, which was very odd, considering she had an engagement ring in her possession – from him.

Libby ground the coriander and cumin in a pan and dry-roasted them over a hot flame. She blended the roasted spices together with the chillies, garlic and onions. Galangal. She hadn't been able to buy any of that, but after looking it up, she decided fresh ginger would do. What else did she need? Lemon, shrimp paste, peanut oil…as she worked, a memory of Robert suddenly appeared in her mind. If they had been closer friends, she would have invited him over to try her new recipe.

After their last encounter, they had parted on a more cordial footing than the previous occasion, but that was before his glamorous cousin Diana had arrived on the scene. Complete with baby, of course. Libby mused over their possible relationship. If Diana had a baby, then wasn't there a possibility of a father for the infant? Libby was astonished over how Robert kept appearing in her thoughts.

After blending the ingredients, she read the next stage in her cookery book. *Place curry paste in a large saucepan, stir over heat until fragrant. Add coconut milk*…the telephone ringing from her living room made her stop. Bother. She really wanted a quiet evening. She didn't want to waste time with idle chat. She put down her wooden spoon and walked through to the other room.

She glanced at the caller's recorded number and was again startled at her reaction to Robert.

"Hello, Robert. How are you? I wasn't expecting you to call." Her heart was racing in her chest as she waited for his reply.

"Libby, I'm fine, thanks, and you? I haven't forgotten about your back door. I don't suppose you've had a chance to get it fixed yet? No? Well, that's good because I've bought a new lock for you."

Libby murmured something about him being 'most kind' as her thoughts whirled around in her head.

"So, if it's convenient, I thought I might call round and fit it for you? How are you fixed this evening?"

Libby thought fast. She had managed to get one part of her chaotic life *almost* in order with Nigel. Did she now want the possibility of being further involved with Robert – in any way – to perhaps screw things up again? So far her life was running true to form. She was hopeless with men and relationships.

"I'm not doing anything much. So yes, that's fine by me."

"Good. When's the best time to come?"

"Have you eaten? If not, why don't you come over now, and we can eat here."

"Libby cooking? Wow! After what you told me in Alfredo's, this I can't miss. What are you going to serve?"

"Um, chicken."

"Fine. I'll pick up some suitable wine. Give me about fifty minutes. See you then."

With mixed thoughts over her sudden change of evening plans, Libby decided she should interrupt her cooking and dashed upstairs to put on something a bit more attractive than the rather scruffy shorts and top she was wearing. She chose a summer dress in a pretty, soft material and picked a pair of sandals that complimented the colour. Light eye shadow and mascara; a soft, pearly lipstick and a squirt of perfume behind her ears. Her newly-washed hair shone from its recent shampooing, and she gave it another flick with her brush. She paused to check her appearance in the mirror and gazed at her reflection. Her eyes shone and her cheeks were slightly flushed.

I don't know why you seem so excited, she said to herself. He's obviously got a temper, and probably has more than one other female in tow. So, we'll make sure this is just a friendly visit. He's here to put a new lock on the door – because he's worried about my safety – and in return, I'm going to treat him to dinner. Nothing else, as I don't want to get involved. Yeah, said another voice as she skipped down the stairs in anticipation.

Chapter 29

One characteristic of Peter's Asperger's syndrome was his acute attention to detail. Since early childhood, he had been fascinated by different technologies. Although he was capable of more, he favoured an easy job where he could be left much to his own devices. Peter preferred to apply his technical mind to his few hobbies, channelling his energies there.

For as long as he could remember, his only hobbies had been amateur dramatics and trainspotting. For Peter, collecting the numbers and names of locomotives seen at railway stations and other vantage points was just the beginning. Ever since he had taken the first steps on his own to a London train station, he had developed a deep and astonishing knowledge about all manner of intricacies where locomotive engines were involved. If anyone cared to ask, he could have easily recited exactly where each and every rivet, nut and bolt that made up each engine was manufactured.

The same could be said of his almost obsessional interest with amateur dramatics, and although he never took to the stage himself, he was a natural with stage make-up and masks. Perhaps this was why he was so concerned about the recent attacks on nurses within Southampton General Hospital.

Peter had been following the newspapers carefully. His mind focused clearly on the initial attacks on nursing staff at St Thomas's Hospital. There had been three vicious attacks on nurses and another attack on a radiographer.

When the first nurse was stalked at Southampton General, she had said, according to the press, she thought her attacker was possibly wearing a mask. The attacker in both locations was believed to be a white male, of medium height, and thin. Peter's main worry was quite simple; if the attacker was wearing a mask, unless a trap was laid and he was caught red-handed, there would never be any hope of him being identified. CCTV was important, but unless a couple of burly policemen happened to be on site at the time, the attacker was unlikely to be caught. They could sift through all the DNA samples they had on record, and it would prove nothing if they didn't already have the attacker's sample. A photograph of the man was needed. Perhaps with all the extra security staff and CCTV, they would catch him.

Peter wondered just what he should do next.

Chapter 30

Robert bolted upstairs to clean his teeth and check his facial stubble. He reckoned he could get away without shaving, and yet maybe Libby may be the type of woman who preferred clean-shaven men. As he shaved, he wondered if he should go the whole hog and splash some of his tangy aftershave on as well. He decided not to in the end. He had to keep things in perspective. This was not a date. He was going to see Libby only to fit a new lock on her door, and for repayment, she was giving him a meal. He wondered on how she would cook the chicken and pondered if it would be better to take on the task of cooking after fitting the lock. She had already told him she wasn't a cook. He grinned at his reflection; he could always get fish and chips on the way home afterwards, if it proved a total disaster! He ran a comb through his hair, changed his mind, and splashed a dab of aftershave on his smooth cheeks. Nothing ventured, nothing gained, he chuckled to himself.

He ran downstairs and hunted for his car keys on the hall table. He found them under a soft toy rabbit belonging to Diana's baby. He poked his head round the living room door and found mother and baby playing on the floor. He concluded there was something nice about having a tiny baby around the place again and was happy to watch them from the doorway. Diana was oblivious, and he grinned as he listened to her ridiculous baby talk.

"I'm off then, Di. I'm not sure what time I'll be back. As I said earlier, Libby is treating me to some of her home cooking, and as I've yet to sample it, I may be home sooner than later! I might well have to settle for fish and chips. What time are you seeing Steph?"

"She's coming round about seven. We're going to watch a DVD after we've put Poppy to bed and then have a glass or two of red wine. It's a treat having so many different wines here. We're a bit limited in Cyprus. Although many are pretty good, Cypriot wines are usually dry and full, so a good Rioja or Bordeaux makes a nice change. Stephanie's bringing a takeaway, as you know."

"Hmm. Sounds like quite a girly night to me. I'm probably doing the right thing going out."

Diana laughed. "You've hardly told me anything about this Libby of yours, you know. I can't remember you ever being quite so tight-lipped before. I'll have to pump Steph for some info."

"She's not 'my Libby'. She's engaged to a surgeon. And I'm actually amazed she's letting me go round there in the first place. I wonder if she cooks for her fiancé. Knowing

Nigel, I doubt it, as he usually has a rod stuck right up his backside."

"Do I hear a hint of jealousy in your voice, dearest coz?" She laughed again at his expression. "Stephanie said you had the hots for Libby"

"Stephanie knows nothing and should keep her nose out of my business. Yes, I do like her as a matter of fact, but we're really not that compatible. We've already had a major argument."

"I wonder what about?" Diana raised her eyebrows at his discomfiture.

"Pack it in. You're not going to practice your amateur sleuthing on me. Keep it for your own murder mysteries back home."

"Aw, come on Robert. You know I won't breathe a word. Besides, since Poppy was born, I've had nothing juicy to get my teeth into since our latest mystery out in Malaysia, and before that we had the murders in Cyprus. So I'm a bit starved of murder mystery *et al.* I was only wondering how you and Libby could already have had—"

"Diana, I must be off. You're as bad as Stephanie – always trying to fix me up. I don't need fixing up with anyone, really I don't, so please forget it. I'm happy as I am."

"Methinks you doth protest too much," she said softly. "Is it still so very bad? So very upsetting to talk about?"

"No. I am over it. I can rationalise now. And having you and baby Poppy here is good for me. I'm enjoying watching you with her. I'd forgotten just how a baby can bring people together, and she's a lovely baby. She's bonnie and happy just like her mother."

"Just like Carole and Morwenna were. Still *are* in your heart. Go on, dear cousin. Have a nice evening with your friend, and I truly hope her food is worth it."

Robert gave a rueful smile as he left Diana sitting on the floor. He meant what he said. The deep, stabbing hurt on finding Morwenna and Carole at the foot of the cliff, with the waves crashing over the car were still very real. Over time, the pain was slowly receding. He would visit the garden of rest tomorrow, where their ashes were sprinkled under Morwenna's favourite flower bushes. He hadn't been for a while, and it was time to pay his respects once again.

He hummed a tune as he walked from his front door and settled himself in his car. He knew telling Di to mind her own business was like waving a red rag to a bull. She would try her utmost to wheedle everything out of him. Besides, with his sister joining her later, he knew what a tenacious pair they were together. He exhaled noisily as he imagined what they would conjure up next. He backed out of his drive and decided to leave them to it. Where certain women were concerned, some things would always be out of his control.

Chapter 31

Stella settled herself onto a settee near the huge window. As she gazed across the panorama in front of her, she couldn't help thinking how clever Nigel was when it came down to finding property that would always increase in value. In the deepening twilight, lights were coming on, spilling their brilliance over the streets and city gardens below; further away, she could see the steaming lights of a cruise ship as she made her way down Southampton Water into the Solent beyond. Nigel always spent time when choosing property. The house in Knightsbridge was one fine example. He had found it in a state of decay during their first years as housemen, and luckily, he had had the foresight to understand and see its potential. Nigel had badgered his father, who was a wealthy Queen's silk, to assist him with the money for the property. Once Nigel had the keys in his hands, he employed an interior designer friend and building company to renovate the place. Now, over a decade later, Nigel stood to make a substantial profit if he ever decided to sell his London home. A few million pounds were not to be sneezed at, and Stella *adored* money. She reckoned Nigel to be worth a thousand times more than when they had first wed, and when the old man St John died, Nigel would inherit the bulk of his estate. For one reason or another, Stella knew she would never relinquish her stake in Nigel.

Stella shifted her weight and tucked her legs under her. She was still wearing the binding on her leg, despite it being all but healed and didn't warrant the large dressing at all. For the time being, Stella chose to keep the bandage in place as it suited her purposes. Nigel was attentive, and she enjoyed having him running around. It afforded her great amusement.

Watching him while he poured generous measures of gin into tall glasses, she wondered about his latest fling with this nurse, Libby. Of course, Stella had made it her business to find out all about her, as she had with his 1001 other relationships over the years. Just because they lived apart, didn't mean Stella had finished with her surgeon husband. She knew she would never have him *totally* to herself, but over the years, she had grown to accept it because she knew he always returned to her in the end. She made sure of that.

"Slice of lime?" he asked, looking over in her direction.

"Yes please, darling. Are you coming to join me over here? This apartment really does have the most marvellous view. Look! Isn't that the new Queen Mary II leaving her berth?"

Nigel crossed the polished wood panelled floor and peered through the glass. "Looks like her. Did you know at the end of November 2011, Southampton will no longer be her registered port?"

Stella shook her head. "No".

"It's changing to Hamilton, Bermuda. Strange to think that Britain once owned many cruising companies, including Cunard, and now doesn't own one. They've all been sold, disbanded, or bought out by other cruising giants."

"Talking of boats, how's your *Tourbillon?* Have you managed to get much sailing in this year? Thanks for the G and T by the way, this lime really gives it a zing," she said, giving Nigel a warm smile as he sat next to her. She shuffled round so that her thigh was resting against his. "It's a bit like your aftershave actually. I recognise it as the one I bought you the last time I was home."

Nigel nodded and returned her smile as he took a sip of his cocktail before replying, "No, regretfully, not nearly enough sailing. I've been frantically busy this summer, not just here but up in town too. Perhaps once the holidays are over, things will calm down, and I can actually do some cruising. I was planning a trip to the Channel Islands, but I had to scupper that idea."

Stella laughed. "But think of the money you're making. Plenty of time for extended cruising once you've retired. Did I tell you my partner in New York has bought a brand new Hinckley and keeps it at the Seawanhaka Corinthian Yacht

Club on Long Island? Have you ever visited there? No? Well I did, last May, and it was fabulous."

"Yes, I have. The club is twinned with The Royal Yacht Squadron at Cowes. Sebastian's a member and I've been with him a couple of times."

"I thought you couldn't stand him the last time I was here."

"No. I just don't like his racing tactics sometimes. He carves up far too tight and takes too many risks."

"And you don't?" Stella replied archly.

Nigel gave her a long look as if he was considering what she really meant. Stella noted his dark expression and decided to change the subject. She didn't want him thinking she had guessed his plan.

"So, are you thinking of dining in or out? If you're intending to eat out, I've been told of a rather splendid little Italian restaurant in the back streets of Southampton. It's called Alfredo's. Do you know it?"

Nigel paused while lifting his glass to his mouth, and Stella could have sworn he looked startled. He shook his head and turned the corners of his mouth down. "No I don't. I've never heard of it."

Chapter 32

Libby couldn't help the skip in her step as she whizzed round her home, ensuring it was tidy and looked inviting. She laid the table for two with her best cutlery and wine glasses. She also decided that, if she was going to make the table look attractive, she would do it properly. After locating a boxed set of snowy-white table linen, she unearthed a couple of silver rings and slipped them over the napkins. Did it look too over the top? she wondered while studying her efforts. Flowers! She needed a small sprig of summer flowers to complete the arrangement.

Having taken a pair of scissors from her kitchen drawer, Libby opened the French windows wide to the balmy evening air, enjoying the sweet scents of summer as she slipped outside. Her roses were still producing beautiful flowers, and she carefully picked a handful of the best creamy-yellow buds she could find. She glanced round her small garden and paused. It was warm enough to eat outside, and she wondered if she should bring the table onto the small patio. Perhaps, again, it was a tad too over the top. Robert was primarily coming over to fit her new lock.

Besides, knowing her luck the weather would change and turn cold.

Taking a last breath of air, she turned to go back indoors and noticed someone standing on the other side of the garden hedge. The side of her garden led to a small cul-de-sac, where there were about half a dozen smart houses. She supposed the person was waiting for someone because she could smell cigarette smoke drifting from that direction. Curious about her stranger, Libby silently moved towards her garden boundary. The hedge was thinner at one end, and she knew where she could part the foliage to get a clearer look beyond. As she edged closer, the figure darted away and made for the road. There was a blare from the horn of a passing vehicle that narrowly missed him. Annoyed because she had failed to see who it was, Libby ran indoors and opened the front door. A bus was pulling into the parking bay and peering through the filmy bus windows, Libby could swear she recognised the figure as he boarded and moved down the length of the bus. Standing on the front doorstep with a puzzled frown on her face, Libby thought she had seen Peter, the hospital porter.

What on earth was he doing down this road? Of course, there was no law to say he shouldn't be here, but Libby felt a shiver run down her spine, especially after the other night. If it was him, why had he been standing so near her flat? Disturbed, Libby closed and bolted the door behind her. She leaned back against the solid wood, closing her eyes, feeling sick with apprehension. Keep calm! she told herself. It's more likely to be a coincidence, and the man just resembled Peter. As her pulse rate slowed down, Libby opened her eyes and stole a look at her watch. It was time to check the kitchen and her cooking. She moved away from the door and gave a scream when the doorbell suddenly burst into life.

Libby put her hand to her throat in fright, then realised her foolishness as the caller was probably Robert. Gathering her wits, she peered through the safety spy-hole and, sure enough, recognised his features.

"What the devil was that scream for?" he asked, when she threw open the door. "Are you all right? You look a bit pale."

Shaking with relief, Libby gave a wan smile and stepped aside as he walked in and closed the door behind him. He was holding a carrier bag in one hand and some sort of workman's satchel-type bag in the other. "Libby?"

She nodded, the lump in her throat threatening to choke her. "I'm fine. I tripped over the rug and I…I nearly knocked the vase off the hall table. I overreacted. Come through to the kitchen."

Robert followed, clutching his bags. "Mmm. Something smells good. Chicken did you say?"

Managing a proper smile, Libby nodded. "That's if it all goes according to the recipe. I'm trying out Thai Green

Curry on you. It's my first attempt, so you're my guinea-pig for the evening."

Robert gave a low whistle. "Not only beautiful but clever too. Thai is probably my favourite food after Italian. Shall I do the door first though? I don't think it'll take too long. The instructions are straight forward."

"It might be better while it's still daylight outside. And I don't know about being clever – you've never tasted my cooking. Would you like a drink?"

"Yes please, a beer if you've got one. It's been pretty hot today and I'm thirsty. I'll make a start on the lock at once."

Libby wandered over to her glasses cupboard and selected a beer tankard. She could have just given him the can but thought he might appreciate a glass. As she poured the beer, she watched him covertly while he worked. Despite his apparent friendliness, she thought she sensed an aloofness about him and then immediately scolded herself, thinking she really was becoming paranoid over the slightest little thing. She turned back to check her cooking while Robert unpacked his bag and produced a substantial-looking lock, which he explained was known as a night latch.

"This should do the job. It's nice and sturdy, much better than that old brass chain that looks like it could pop if someone put their shoulder to it," he said later, when he stood back to admire his handiwork. "The lock is actually slightly stiff and will need a bit of getting used to. I've greased it, but try it and see."

Robert showed Libby how to set and reset the lock. He was right, the lock was a bit difficult, but she said she would soon get used to it. "Knowing it's there makes me feel heaps safer. Thank you," she said, after trying it out a few times. "Okay, I reckon I've got the hang of it now. So, shall we have our dinner? It's all ready apart from the rice, which is nearly done. I thought we'd eat in if that's all right? They did forecast rain later and knowing my luck…"

~~~~~

Robert sat back in his chair with a satisfied look upon his face. "Libby, I have to say that was delicious, especially for someone who professes not to cook. Next time, it's my turn."

Libby smiled. "Are you sure? You're not just saying that? Usually I'm rubbish when it comes to cooking."

He laughed. "Of course I am. Believe me, I wouldn't lie to you. What would be the point? No, it was scrumptious!"

"Let's take the rest of the wine outside shall we? The rain's held off, and it's still a warm evening."

"Good idea. I'll uncork the other bottle as we've nearly finished this one. I hope red is okay? I want to talk to you anyway.

Libby looked surprised at his remark. "That sounds ominous, what about?"

"Now, I don't want to pry or upset you, but are you going to tell me about your intruder? Or am I going to be the last person you inform?" Robert raised his eyebrows, while tasting a sip of the new wine.

Libby flushed. "So who told you? I bet I can guess. He never could keep quiet."

"Isn't it just as well? When were you going to let me know, if at all?"

"Robert—" she said, turning away in embarrassment. "I promise I was going to tell you this evening. I've been so busy, and I guess I just forgot. When did Jem speak to you?"

"The very day your co-sister, Lisa, told him. Libby, you must realise we're all concerned about you. Especially Lisa – she says you've not been yourself lately. Are you still having odd feelings?"

Thinking back to just before Robert's arrival and her scare after seeing that man loitering outside, Libby hesitated. The police hadn't really believed her as nothing had been stolen or disturbed, and she had little else to back up her strange feelings. Even so, she realised Robert would be as mad as hell if she kept this thing to herself.

"Ye–es. That is, something strange happened just before you arrived."

Robert immediately looked grim. "Let's go into the garden then, shall we? I get the feeling I should be sitting down."

Libby followed him, and they sat on a bench side by side. The evening was calm and the sweet scent from the night stocks hung in the air. Traffic noises were muted and Libby could almost imagine they were in the country.

"It's nothing really. I just had a bit of a surprise. I thought I saw one of the hospital porters, Peter, hanging around outside earlier; immediately before you arrived, actually. I thought you might have seen him. I was in the garden and happened to glance through the bushes over there," she said, indicating with her hand. "And there was this man having a smoke, whom I thought looked very much like Peter. I couldn't see absolutely clearly, as the hedge was in the way, even the part where it's thinner. But it's strange. I'm sure he doesn't live near here, and I've never seen him around before. Anyway, he suddenly dashed across the road. I thought it was because he realised I'd seen him, and he jumped onto a bus going towards the city centre. Am I being stupid?" she asked in a soft voice.

Robert didn't answer immediately. Instead he took one look at her miserable face and put his arm around her. "Libby, I don't think anyone can be stupid where safety is concerned. Look. You're a single woman living on her own. There have been some horrendous attacks on women lately, and they've all been nurses. I know the incidents have all happened in the vicinity of the hospital, but who knows?

With this madman, he could be moving into new territory. I don't want to scare you, but I believe you have to be extra careful. Now, you don't know for sure if it was this Peter. Even if it was, his being there may be entirely innocent. We can inform the police, if you like. Would you like to do that?"

"I got the distinct feeling the police didn't believe me about my intruder, especially as nothing was disturbed. And yes, I've nothing else to go on other than some odd feelings. I don't know Peter well, but Lisa does, and she says he's harmless. He suffers from Asperger's Syndrome and is clever but socially challenged. She says he'd never hurt a fly."

Robert looked pensive. "Yes, well, that's as maybe. I think mentioning it to the local cop shop won't hurt. I think we ought to tell Jem though. I'm sure he'll know Peter a lot better than you do because he'll have more contact with him down in Accident Centre. Don't look so worried, this is what friends are for. By the way, what about your fiancé? Where does Nigel fit into all this? Is he around or up in town? And how much have you told him?"

Robert's comforting arm made Libby feel safe. It was warm and reassuring, yet there was something that was oddly familiar. She stole a look at Robert.

"Ah! I thought you'd get round to asking me about him."

~~~~~

"So, we're having a sort of break from each other. It makes sense if you think about it," Libby said, while refreshing their glasses.

"Sorry, you've completely lost me. You say you've hardly spoken to Nigel lately because he *lost* his mobile, which coincidentally was handed in to the police once it had been found at the hospital. Then next you tell me your fiancé has his ex-wife staying with him, and you're putting moving in with him on hold. But you've not yet told him anything about your intruder, let alone your scare earlier this evening? Have I got all that right? Libby, I despair of you."

She stared at him. "Why? Oh, I see. Or at least I think I do." She began to laugh, and then to her embarrassment, her laughter turned to sobs. To her horror, she couldn't stop the tears sliding down her face making black runnels from her mascara.

~~~~~

"Better now?"

"She nodded, took a deep breath, and tried a tremulous smile. "Sorry. I'm such a fool. I *feel* such a fool."

"Libby, there's no need to apologise. You've been through a hell of a lot over the last few weeks. We all make mistakes, me included." Robert took a sip of his brandy and gestured that Libby should do the same.

"You're right, of course. I truly think everything has got on top of me. What I haven't told you yet is where Nigel and I stand, and when I do tell you, you'll probably think I'm quite barmy."

Robert looked interested at her words, and if Libby had known him better, she would have thought he was holding his breath. "Go on, try me."

"I've finally come to the conclusion we aren't suited. Ever since I came out of hospital, things have felt odd – I've mentioned this before. What I didn't tell you was when I first woke up in hospital and found Nigel sitting there – at first a total stranger to me – he immediately said I was his fiancé. When I looked at my hand and noticed my bare fingers, he explained my engagement ring was in the jewellers being resized. Robert, I…I don't actually believe we were ever engaged. I think it's all something he's made up, and I don't know why. I think he does love me in his way, but I've never truly felt completely cherished. Do you understand? Am I going mad?"

Libby raised a woeful face, and Robert took one of her hands in his, giving her fingers a reassuring squeeze. "No, I don't for one minute. I know you won't thank me for reminding you of this, but very early on I said there was something about Nigel that disturbed me. Remember that day when we'd been sailing and we argued over him? He never rang true somehow, and as for leaving you so much on your own lately, well what on earth has he been doing? Oh, I know he's an important surgeon with his Harley Street practice, and he's on various hospital boards, but he's not very *lovable* is he? And now you're saying his ex-wife is staying with him. Why? Does she still have a hold on him? And something else Jem said troubled me too."

Libby stole another look in his direction. "Oh? What's that? You seem to have got to know Jem rather well."

"This was originally from Lisa, actually. She told Jem that Nigel had a key to this place. Now, I realise who you give a key to is your business, but have you thought about it, truly thought about the implication of someone else having access to your home? I'm sure Nigel is honest, and there's nothing to really concern us, but you had an intruder recently. He could have mentioned to someone in passing that he had the key to your place, so that he could pick up some of your things while you were in hospital. He could have left it lying around, possibly at the hospital or some place, and anyone could have put two and two together. Okay, it's a long shot, but all I'm saying is strange things happen sometimes through a chain of events that we know nothing about. Good heavens!" Robert gave a sudden dry chuckle.

"What?"

"I've begun to sound like my cousin, Diana, from Cyprus. You remember I mentioned her to you."

Libby nodded, wishing she could stop the sudden flush from stealing over her cheeks. How well she remembered that embarrassing episode in her life.

"She's the one I saw you with down at West Quay the other day."

It was Robert's turn to nod. "What I've never mentioned is she's a bit of an amateur sleuth as well as being a writer. She sees mysteries in almost everything and loves working out why people behave as they do. I bet if I mentioned you to her, she would know exactly what was happening here."

"I'm not sure I want someone I haven't met knowing all my business," Libby retorted.

"Of course, I'm being ill-mannered and jumping to conclusions. There may be absolutely nothing to worry about. But I'll say this: I am going to get Jem to arrange a meeting with the porter. A pub will do nicely, I think! He'll know more about him, Peter you said his name was, I believe? Perhaps Jem can ask him in a roundabout way if he was here earlier today and if so, why. That'll solve one mystery, don't you think? I'm only sorry I missed seeing him, and then I would have known what he looks like."

"Please tell Jem to be careful. I wouldn't want anyone being accused of something if they're innocent. If it wasn't him, then I'm going to look very silly, and the more I think about it, the less sure I am." Libby looked troubled.

"Of course. Just leave it to us, and try and stop worrying. Thank you for trusting me with this. Perhaps we should have trusted each other more earlier on, and then we wouldn't have had any misunderstandings. It's my turn to trust you with a secret of my own. I know Stephanie hasn't told you as she knows my feelings over this, but I was married some time ago. I was very happy with my wife, Morwenna, and our baby daughter, Carole. Unfortunately, they were both killed in a dreadful accident some years back. I rarely mention it, and it's only now since meeting you and having Diana and her daughter, Poppy, to stay that I feel I can speak about it. When this is all over I'll tell you everything, but for the moment please bear with me." He looked quite sad and then seemed to pull himself together as he continued.

"Now my girl, time is getting on. Would you like to come back to my place for a night or two? Diana was staying with a friend, but she's with me now and has the bedroom you slept in after Stephanie and Graham's party, but there is another little bedroom. I'm sure she wouldn't mind having the baby in with her."

Libby felt overwhelmed by what Robert had just disclosed, but she wasn't surprised. She thought there had always been something simmering beneath his usual good temper. She decided to play it down and let him tell her more when he felt able to.

"Robert, I'm sorry. I never knew. And of course, please tell me more when you're ready. I'll always be here to listen. As for staying with you, I am tempted, really I am, but I need to learn to stand on my own feet. Thank you for your kind offer, and thanks for all you've done here today. I'm okay, especially with the solid lock you've just fitted, so I'll be all right. Everything will be locked up tight as soon as you've gone home," she reassured him. Libby gave him a huge smile, trying to show she was full of confidence.

Robert studied her closely before replying. His eyes looked soft and gentle, caring even. "Well, if I can't persuade you, then I'll have to accept your word. When did you say you were going to tell Nigel it was all over between you?"

Libby sighed. "I didn't, but believe me, I'm going to tell him as soon as possible."

Robert stood up to go, giving her a long, searching look. "You know there's nothing I'd like more than to take you in my arms and really look after you," he said in a soft voice, while holding a hand up as she tried to interrupt. "But in view of the fragile state you're in, it wouldn't be fair – to either of us. When this has all settled down, you'd look back and think I'd taken advantage of you. I'd like to mean something to you, Libby, but only when you've finally got Nigel out of your system. Until then, I'll always be here for you, but simply as a friend."

He gave her a quick kiss on the cheek. "Well, goodnight then. All I can say to you is good luck, and I hope he takes it well."

Libby sat in her darkened sitting room long after Robert had left. She felt as if she had swallowed something hard that had lodged itself in her throat. It was just as well Robert had left when he did. If he had stayed any longer, she knew she would have invited him to stay the night at *her* place. What she had said was true about being tempted to stay with him. She felt as if she was on a piece of string and being pulled first one way and then the other. Robert had been so full of understanding this evening, and she had enjoyed being comforted with his arms around her. She wondered about his dead wife and child. How tragic to have lost both in an accident. She hoped, when the time came, she could help him over his grief.

If only Nigel would react the same way when she explained how she truly felt about him, but somehow she doubted it.

Libby shivered as if someone had walked over her grave.

Chapter 33

As Robert drove away, he felt frustrated and deeply troubled. He wished he had arrived early enough to have caught sight of whomever it was near Libby's flat. Robert wasn't entirely convinced it was Peter because she looked and acted as if she was suffering from immense strain. Despite being a regular visitor to the hospital during the last year, Robert didn't know Peter at all. He was just another anonymous worker in hospital clothing, and yet something Libby had said rung a bell. He wondered again if it had been Peter, or was Libby imagining things? The main question was, why was Peter there in the first place? What did he know? Robert decided he needed to talk to Jem about him, if only to erase any suspicion. If Jem felt uncomfortable with his suggestion, then he could very quickly get in touch with the police.

Robert put his foot down on the accelerator in anger. Peter could surely only have come to warn Libby about something. Robert wondered just what the something was, and had Peter seen *him tonight?* Muttering to himself, Robert swore. More people meant more problems to overcome, but there was one good thing that had happened today. Libby had finally decided to give Nigel the elbow. Robert really didn't know what she had seen in the creep in the first place.

Chapter 34

The next day was very typical of an English summer. Libby drew back her curtains to a grey sky, swollen with dark and heavy-looking clouds. Vehicles were moving along her road with full headlights on. The noise which had wakened her was car tyres as they swished over the soaking tarmac. She groaned and once more asked herself why hadn't she sold up and moved abroad to live? Most hospitals in the world were crying out for experienced nurses, and sometimes she wished desperately to get away from weeks and weeks of awful weather. It wasn't that she loathed the odd wet day. It was just that very often one wet day let to another and another.

With this depressing consideration in her mind she turned her thoughts to Nigel. He had insisted on coming round to see her later that day despite all her efforts to put him off. She knew she was being bamboozled into seeing him, but he had sounded kind and loving over the telephone. She had agreed meekly because she had yet to tell him it was all over.

Now, she needed to get through the day at work, drive home and await his arrival. What a bugger, she thought as she dashed into her bathroom to take a shower. She only hoped he would understand they were not suited after all, and they could carry on as just good friends. Somehow though, she had a niggle of a suspicion that things would *not* go her way at all. After towelling her hair dry, she gave a shiver as she put on clean clothes. Today was so unlike summer. Cold, wet and dreary – maybe she would look into working abroad after all. Perhaps if she met Robert's cousin, Diana, she would ask her about Cyprus. 300 days of sunshine a year? Now *that* was worth it!

~~~~~

The morning flew by with a full quota of theatre cases. Both Lisa and Libby were working the afternoon shift together, and as the afternoon drew to a close, Lisa finally asked Libby why she was acting like a cat on a hot tin roof.

"I've never seen you like this before. Is everything all right?" Lisa asked when there was a lull in the frantic activity.

"Actually, yes and no. I've finally made up my mind. Nigel's not the man of my dreams, and I'm going to tell him tonight. So I'm a bit hot and bothered about it all. You know what he's like. He's quite capable of throwing all his surgeon's instruments out of the pram!"

She looked at Lisa whose face broke into a broad grin. "Are you? Uh-ho! I don't envy you, my girl." She gave her a quick hug. "Don't worry. I'm sure he'll see reason once you've talked things over. He's intelligent, and he's hardly likely to murder you! Ring me when he's gone, if you want to talk."

"I might just do that, depending on how he reacts and what time he leaves." She gave a sheepish grin. "This time tomorrow, I'll be a free woman again. All I need to do is work out what I want from life. Do I want to be married and settled down or live on my own, as it seems I'm destined to do? I might even go and work abroad for a stint."

Lisa peered into her friend's face. "Don't be like that. You *will* meet someone. You can hardly fail not too with your looks. Look at your pilot friend. He was smitten when he first met you, and don't tell me you weren't interested. Once this is all over, you can always decide whether to have a relationship with him. Do ring me tonight once Nigel's gone. I won't sleep until I know it's all settled."

"Okay, as long as it's not too late. Pregnant ladies need their rest," she said, giving her a gentle poke in the stomach. "Have you felt it move yet?"

Lisa laughed. "No, it's far too early! By the way, have you told Jem about Nigel yet?"

"Yes. He knows everything and was quite un-PC about it."

Lisa giggled. "Good. Jem knows what is best for you, even if you don't. Oh look, there's Nigel now." She moved away from Libby towards the surgeon who had just walked up to the nurses' station. "Good afternoon."

"Afternoon, Lisa. Libby – just to tell you that unless anything important crops up, I'll be over about eight tonight."

Chapter 35

Peter glanced nervously around him before looking Jem properly in the eye, as if making sure there was no one else to overhear their conversation.

"Relax, Peter. There's no one near us. The pub's pretty empty at the moment. Most people have gone home for the night. Would you prefer to sit further away from the door? The table in the corner near the inglenook fireplace is empty."

Peter looked relieved and nodded as Jem stood up indicating they should move. "Come on then. Let's get settled. Fancy a pint? I'll get these."

Jem wandered over to the bar, making a comment to someone he knew on his way. He leaned on the bar while the barmaid pulled a couple of pints and then weaved his way back through the low tables to where Peter sat waiting. Although Jem knew Peter well, there were times when Peter was reluctant to talk about anything, let alone something as sensitive as Jem thought he had to impart. So far, all Jem knew was that Peter had something on his mind, and he presumed it concerned Libby.

"I need to tell you Libby's friend Robert is joining us, Peter. He should be here soon. Now, although you don't know him, Libby does, and she trusts him. We want to ask you a couple of questions, if that's all right."

Peter sat and stared at Jem with a puzzled expression on his face. "Why?" he eventually asked.

"Well, Libby thought she saw you at her place the other night. If it was you, she wondered what you were doing there and why."

Peter's eyes darted around the pub, and he swallowed before replying. "I was going to talk to her, but I lost my nerve." He picked up a beer mat and began fiddling with it.

Jem spoke with a gentle voice as he once again addressed a clearly anxious Peter. "Why was that? Libby's nice and friendly. She wouldn't do anything to spite you."

"I wanted to warn her about that man." He kept his face averted, turning the mat over and over in his hand.

Jem eyes narrowed. "Which man is that? Do you mean Robert or someone else? Tell me."

"That night that little nurse was attacked. She looked like a lot like Libby, and I got confused. He might have a thing about blonde nurses."

Jem was patient as he waited for Peter to explain more. When he didn't, he spoke in a soft, low voice. "Peter, what exactly did you see? Was it the attacker? Did you see him attack the nurse that night?

"Not exactly." Peter paused and frowned as if remembering what had happened. Eventually he looked up and tossed the beer mat back onto the table. "I wasn't meant to be there, but I came back that night to fetch a magazine from my locker. That's when I saw him – as I took a shortcut past the teaching block. I know all the doctors here. I've got a good memory for faces, and I know he wasn't one of the regular ones." Peter rocked his chair back and forth, alternating between the front and back legs.

Jem nodded. "Indeed you have – one of the best memories I've ever known. Go on."

"Well, I wondered why he was there, you see. When we have locums they generally work during the day. There was no reason why he should have been in that part of the hospital either, as there's nothing there at night. But that's not what concerned me."

"No? So what was it then?"

"He was wearing a wig and stage make-up. Not a mask as some people seem to think."

Jem stared at him. "Are you sure?"

"Positive. I know all the colours actors wear on their faces. I'm very good at making up at my drama group, and everyone asks me to do them when there's a production on. I've used Ben Nye make-up for years because it is proper theatrical make-up. Their kits contain expert components that produce professional results on the stage. I won't work with anything else. You see, Nye's formulas go on velvety smooth, and they stay on for hours. This man was wearing a blended crème based foundation with crème eye shadow and lip colour. He's not as good as me in applying it, as his eyebrows didn't look quite right. I thought they were a bit too thin."

"What about the wig?"

"It looked like a standard issue from any department store. Dark hair, quite short and he'd used a medium to tan foundation on his skin."

"How can you be sure he was wearing all this?"

Peter shrugged. "I just know. People say I have an eye for detail and this was definitely someone wearing stage make-up."

"Not a mask then? That's what the police think."

"No. I'm almost 100 per cent sure this was simply stage make-up." Peter tilted his chair back and stole a look at the nearby window.

Jem nodded as he listened. He believed Peter. He may have been considered as an odd fellow to get to know, but he had always been honest with Jem. He was about to ask Peter another question, when he let his chair drop back to stand on all four legs and suddenly stood up. Jem sat back in surprise.

"What's the matter?"

"I...ah. I just remembered I'm supposed to be somewhere else. I...I'm sorry, but I can't stay to meet Libby's friend. Just tell her I am sorry I surprised her like that. I never meant to. I was going to tell her to be careful, but it doesn't matter now as you can."

Jem was left sitting with his mouth slightly open at Peter's rapid departure. It was the oddest thing. Was it possible Peter didn't want to meet Robert and if so, why not?

Chapter 36

Nigel arrived home from the hospital early in the evening. His theatre list that afternoon had been cut down for once, and with no afternoon clinic, he had found time to dictate his notes for his secretary so he could leave late that afternoon. Traffic was light as he sped down the dual carriageway in his Porsche, and he contemplated his forthcoming date with Libby. It seemed ages since they had enjoyed an evening in each other's company, and he was looking forward to it. He would take a quick shower, change into some comfortable clothes, and pass an hour or so with Stella before leaving his apartment.

The only problem he could foresee was when he eventually explained to Stella that he was going out – alone – and visiting Libby. Having Stella stay with him had its own good moments. Despite any rancour during their early married years, Nigel considered time a great healer, and these days they got on much better. They had actually rekindled past mutual interests, and as he had thought many times during the past week or so, Stella now often took the lead during their sexual activity.

It all boiled down to sex, he thought, as he geared down on approaching his apartment block. When they were at university together, their sexual relationship had been one of a common healthy appetite. During the years when they were married and both were pursuing their careers, Nigel sensed a cooling and waning on Stella's part and turned towards extra marital activity among their joint friends, colleagues and quite often his patients. Nigel found Stella's friends and colleagues to be easy targets. They were often unattached and with healthy sexual cravings of their own. His patients were often more difficult to seduce, but over the years Nigel had found an easy, if prohibited, way round that. He wasn't a qualified doctor for nothing.

Having great sex with Stella was not what Nigel was after. He appreciated having her all right, but because she was free and available, there wasn't the challenge that he so enjoyed. Neither was it illegal.

He parked the car and made his way over to the lift. He clutched a bouquet of summer lilies: tall, wicked-looking spikes with an exotic and heady perfume. Stella adored presents of any sort, and Nigel hoped the simple gift would go half-way to placating her once he explained he needed to go out. If not, he thought with a shrug of the shoulders, then it was too bad. Despite their newfound rapport, Stella wasn't what he needed that evening.

She must have been watching from the living room window. Before he found time to insert his key, she threw open the door and exclaimed with pleasure on catching sight of the flowers.

"Darling, how wonderful! After roses, lilies are always my favourite. How are you? Had a good day?" She enveloped him in a waft of scent and kissed him full on the mouth. He suppressed a laugh as he contemplated what her reaction would have been if he had said they were not for her but for Libby. She was dressed in a short red skirt showing inches of curvy thigh and a skimpy, almost see-through, top.

"Not too bad. It's good to finish early. I could do with a drink though."

"Come through while I fix us one. What'll you have – a whisky or gin?"

"To tell you the truth, I'd like a beer. There's some in the bottom of the fridge."

Nigel dumped his case in the hall and followed Stella towards the kitchen. He noticed she had prepared a tray of canapés and immediately felt a little guilty because of what he was about to tell her.

"They look good. Are they for us or are you expecting others?" he said, indicating the display.

"Silly, of course they're just for us. I'd have told you if we were expecting company." She snuggled nearer as she handed him his beer, her unfettered, full breasts brushing against his arm. "I thought we'd stay in for once and forego dinner out. I'm going to cook fillet steak for us. How does that sound, darling?"

"It sounds wonderful," he said, taking the beer and walking through to the living room. "Unfortunately, I'll have to cry off as I'm going out tonight." He crossed over to the huge picture window glancing down at the scene below.

Stella joined him, pouting at his words. "Oh Nigel. Can't it wait? I was so looking forward to having a quiet evening in. We've been out to so many restaurants, and I wanted to play the little wife for you tonight."

Nigel smiled, knowing full well what she had in mind. At any other time it would have been appealing. How on earth was he going to tell her just who he was seeing? He tensed. This was becoming ridiculous, he was an adult. She knew about Libby. She had known about her almost from the first time they had gone out together. What was the point in being divorced if Stella still acted as if they were still married?

"Sorry, darling. I know you've gone to a lot of trouble, but business can't be helped. Tell you what. We'll have the canapés, and I'll leave here as late as I can. How about that? Say about seven thirty?" he said in a smooth voice while casting a quick look at his Rolex. "That gives us a nice relaxing couple of hours, hmm?"

"I suppose if it *is* work, then I can't begrudge you the time." She gave a dramatic sigh. "It doesn't matter. I can always go over what I'm delivering tomorrow."

"Of course. Your paper on '*Caesarean section for the primigravida mother and the psychological ramifications*'. I'm looking forward to your lecture. It's surprising, as in the States, Caesarean rates are actually falling, yet here in the UK, they're considering allowing first-time mothers the choice of either a C-section or a natural birth. I would have thought it would be the other way round."

Nigel wanted to draw her away from the real reason he was going out that night. Being a coward, he preferred an easy life, and if Stella thought he was meeting a work buddy, then so much the better. "Come and sit down, tell me all about *your* day." He patted the seat next to him on the sofa and drew her down. "We've got plenty of time."

~~~~~

Gunning the Porsche down the road, Nigel knew he was going to be late. After two glasses of chilled Chablis and a fat marijuana joint, Stella had become been wildly amorous. Once she sat astride him, and he realised she wasn't wearing any panties, he knew he was lost. He had been aroused at once, and as she ground herself down with complete and utter abandon onto him, he ejaculated within minutes. Relaxed after the sex, it was hard to drag himself towards the bedroom and shower. Stella was becoming a real sex fiend, and he almost expected her to follow him into the tiled wet room and demand he make passionate love to her once again. He tore off his remaining few clothes and stepped under the hot water, a fully-pressurised jet playing down on his head.

He was going to get away with it but only just – Stella was ugly when jealous. For some reason, she didn't recognise him and Libby as an item. Initially, when Nigel had tried to explain that they were going to live together permanently, Stella either changed the subject or laughed.

"How many times have I heard you say that, my love? You always return to me. You've been shagging your way through the women of the world ever since I first met you. But it never means anything because you never get them to say 'yes' and agree to move in with you, so you always stay home. Darling, it hardly matters now. I'm well used to your little games. So let's stop pretending, eh?"

How many times had he come near to it? Really near? He tried to remember, and the years clouded his mind. He couldn't remember whom he had planned his life with. This time though, he was going to make it with Libby. He patted the pocket of his jacket, making sure he had remembered to bring that item that would make tonight extra special. The song was still going through his head as he walked up her path to the front door to her ground-floor flat, "*You're mine, you belong to me, you, I will never free you, you're here with me to stay, you're mine, you are mine completely.*"

He rapped smartly on her door and turned round to look at her tiny front garden. He couldn't remember which one it had been, but one of his earlier loves had been just like Libby. He remembered her short blonde hair and her slim, well-toned body. She loved gardens too; and she was a nurse. He frowned as he tried to think more clearly...in fact most of his serious loves had been blonde and...nurses. He smiled. One could say he had a real thing about blonde nursing staff.

The sound of a bolt being pushed back made him turn to face the door, and there she stood. His Libby! His darling girl!

"Nigel, you're here."

He smiled as deep a smile as he could, briefly wondering why she looked so pale and tense. "Hello, darling, sorry I'm late. I'm so glad we've finally managed to get an evening together. Are you going to invite me in? I don't really want to kiss you on the doorstep in front of the whole neighbourhood."

Libby stood aside as he walked into her home. She cast a wild look back out at the near street, but it stood empty. There was no one around that she could see.

Chapter 37

Jem couldn't understand it. First Peter had bolted from the pub like a rabbit from its hole, and now Robert had just phoned to say he couldn't make it after all. Robert didn't even pause long enough to ask whether he had found anything out either. Frustrated, Jem downed his unfinished pint, strode over to the bar and ordered another.

"It's nearly time, mate," the barman said. "But seeing as I know ya, just remember you bought this pint ten minutes ago, see? I don't want to lose me licence. What happened to your friend? He left rather sudden like, didn't he?"

"Mmm. Suddenly remembered he had to be somewhere else. Never mind, I'll see him tomorrow at work, and we can finish our conversation then."

The barman nodded and carried on drying his glasses, chatting up the barmaid with his easy banter while she rang up the till for that night's takings.

Jem finished his pint in record time and slapped his glass down on the bar. "See you," he called and made for the exit. The fresh tangy air from the Hamble River hit him as he wandered over to his car and unlocked the door. The night was calm and as black as a tar pit. *I wonder why Peter ran off like that, he mused. One minute we were talking perfectly naturally, or as naturally as you could with Peter and the next, he was off like a whippet.*

Jem concentrated on what they had been saying. He couldn't remember saying anything inflammatory. Peter had been looking out of the window, balancing on two chair legs like a kid. Then suddenly, wham, he was off.

Jem pondered over the evening some more. Had Peter seen something or someone outside the pub to catch his attention? Or had he simply wanted to get away and be on his own? He shook his head. No, something triggered Peter's reaction. What had he seen that was so important that it made him run off like that? A shiver ran down Jem's spine.

Chapter 38

The house was in complete darkness when Robert arrived except for a dim porch light. He let himself in and moved quietly down the hallway into the kitchen. Feeling around the wall, he felt for the switch and was rewarded when the kitchen was flooded in bright light. The clock on the cooker said it was getting on for midnight, and he wasn't surprised finding the house deserted at this hour. Diana wasn't a night owl, and she escaped to bed far earlier than before Poppy's birth.

Since her arrival, he had become used to the kitchen's different odours. Diana enjoyed cooking as much as he did, and they both relished in trying out new recipes on each other. Tonight had been no exception. Robert could still smell the aroma left over from a duck dish she had experimented with. The flavour had been both aromatic and delicate, and Robert found himself wishing his long departed Morwenna could have been there sharing in the fun. He stifled a sigh. For the first time since his family's horrific accident, he felt he was finally coming to terms with life as it now was. Once upon a time, if anyone had suggested that having another woman and her baby sharing his house would be beneficial, he would have laughed in their face. Now he was quite sure Diana and Poppy were balm for his deeply hidden anguish.

Meeting Libby was something else, and he found her proximity disturbing. Thinking of Libby, he turned his thoughts to the evening. He felt bad that he had let Jem down by not meeting him at the pub. Under the circumstances it couldn't be helped. He wondered if Peter had known or seen anything perhaps.

"I thought I heard you come in. Are you making hot chocolate by chance?"

Lost in thought, Robert jumped and turned at the sound of Diana's voice behind him.

"Jesus, Diana, you move like a cat, I didn't hear a thing."

"Sorry. Steve complains about that too. Well, are you? Or shall I do it?" She wandered into the room wearing a cotton knee-length nightdress and nothing on her feet.

"Aren't you cold?" he said, moving over to the cupboard for the tin of chocolate and a carton of milk from the fridge.

"Not really, my feet are a bit. Did you have a nice evening? Who were you meeting? Someone called Jeremy or something."

"Jem, and no, I didn't actually meet him in the end. I got stuck at the base. By the time I managed to get away, it wasn't worth the trouble driving down to Hamble. How do you like this? Extra sugar?"

"Certainly not. A girl has to look after her figure, especially after giving birth. I put on pounds, and I've only just got down to my pre-preggers weight and size, although I have changed shape a bit according to Steve." She grinned as she went and perched on a kitchen stool by the breakfast table.

"You look okay to me," Robert said, eyeing her from where he stood. "Morwenna got her figure back pretty quickly too, if I remember rightly."

"She was a lovely size to start with. I'm a bigger girl all round." She laughed. "So what's new?"

"Nothing."

She sniffed. "Pooh, Robert. Don't forget I'm the actress in the family. What are you hiding?"

He stiffened while adding chocolate to the two brightly-coloured mugs he had lifted down from a shelf and turned to meet her gaze.

"I was just thinking of Libby, that's all. You know she has this knack for getting herself into trouble. Take this so-called fiancé of hers, Nigel. She told me the other night they're having a break from each other. Well, listen to this too. Her *fiancé* has his ex-wife staying with him. Libby's putting on hold moving in with him, and she's not told him anything about her intruder! I despair!"

Diana was silent as she let him carry on.

"She's finally come to the conclusion they're not suited – at long last. That's not all. Apparently, ever since she came out of hospital, things have felt odd to her. She's told me that before. But what she didn't tell me was, when she first woke up in hospital, she found Nigel sitting there at her bedside. She thought he was a total stranger until he claimed she was his fiancée. When she tried to protest and noticed she didn't have an engagement ring, he argued it was in the jewellers being resized. She doesn't actually believe they were ever engaged. She's come to the conclusion it's something he's made up. I tell you, Diana, it's bloody spooky."

"It does sound suspicious."

"Nigel had a key to her place at one time. He allegedly needed it to take her some clothes when she was in hospital. What if he took a copy? Could *he* be her intruder? And now the latest is, she thought she saw some porter called Peter hanging around her house the other evening. That's what Jem was doing this evening when I was supposed to be meeting him. He was going to tactfully put a few questions to the porter."

"Tactfully? What about the police?"

"Well, there's the rub. You see, the porter is apparently a nice, harmless character who suffers from a form of

Asperger's Syndrome. He keeps himself to himself and enjoys a quiet life with his trainspotting and amateur dramatics."

She frowned. "Amateur dramatics? Does he perform on stage then? That sounds strange, as most Aspergers like a solitary life with no fuss and bother."

"No, I don't think so. His forte is stage make-up. He's a whizz at disguise—"

They both looked at each other in shocked silence. They had both heard and read the news reports concerning the hospital attacker and his assault on nurses.

"Stage make-up. What if…? No, it couldn't be. Surely someone would have thought about this before? Besides, Jem says he's harmless," said Robert.

Diana pursed her lips while she thought before replying. "And what *did* Jem find out tonight do you suppose? It'll be interesting when you ask him."

Robert glanced down at his watch. "It's a bit late to ring him now. I know he's on an early tomorrow. Look, there's nothing we can do now until the morning. Let's call it a night and we'll talk to him then. I think I'll finish my chocolate in bed. I'm bushed."

She put her head on one side as she studied him. "Mmm, you do look a bit jaded. By the way, why are your jeans all muddy around the bottom? It looks like you fell into a puddle."

Robert looked down at his feet and saw that she was right. "I took the opportunity to visit *Caterina* while I was down at Hamble. I must have stepped in some water then. There's a high tide at the moment, and the sea was well over the wall in places. I'll say goodnight then."

Chapter 39

"So, when Stella showed up, there was nothing I could do about it except have her stay with me in town."

Nigel sprawled on Libby's sofa, looking very relaxed and evidently savouring the red Rioja wine in his glass. Listening to his explanation about the past couple of weeks' comings and goings, Libby wondered if he was as laid back as he appeared to be. There was a tautness about his face and eyes that she didn't remember being there before. He looked as if he had lost some weight too. Libby felt a pang of guilt. Despite all her good intentions, perhaps she was being too harsh with him. It couldn't be easy having your ex-wife turn up and not be cordial to her, especially when their work involved a certain amount of commitment and involvement between them. She knew all about the famous psychiatrist, Stella, who was also an eminent professor in her field.

"So, does Stella stay with you often?" she heard herself say and not really knowing why she was asking the question. It wasn't as if she was jealous.

Nigel paused as if considering whether to tell her the truth or not, and Libby thought she caught a trace of reddening around the tips of his ears. "To tell you the truth, she does rather impose upon me. These past few years, she's made such a name for herself on both sides of the Atlantic that she's constantly to-ing and fro-ing between England and the States. She doesn't seem to understand that we are finally divorced or that my London house and Southampton apartment are my own. She sometimes turns up without giving me good notice or, on occasions, without letting me know. I have explained to her about you – about us."

Libby felt her stomach flip over. She had to tell Nigel how she felt today. "And?"

"She understands how I feel about you and that we want to be together. As she's spending so much time over here now, I'm going to encourage her to buy her own place. I don't mind her using the London one, but I'd much prefer to have the Southampton one just for us. She's only here for a few more days, she said, and I suggest you move in once she's gone. Darling Libby, I can't wait!" He caught Libby's hand in his own and raised it wrist side uppermost to his lips. "It'll be so good. You do realise I've never lived with anyone else except Stella before, don't you?" He caressed her hand with his fingers, the rhythm almost hypnotic by his touch.

Libby caught her breath, wondering how she could tell Nigel she wasn't moving anywhere. His attitude was beginning to annoy her. Did he think she was really that stupid? It was obvious there was still something between

Faith Mortimer

them. Nobody in their right mind – amongst her circle of friends anyway – regularly shared a house once separated or divorced.

"Actually, Nigel, about me moving in with you, I'm sorr—"

"Darling, shall I get us another drink?" Nigel gave her hand a final stroke and stood up. "Another glass of wine?" He put his hand into his jacket pocket as if looking for something.

Relieved to be given a moment to recollect her thoughts and gather courage, Libby nodded. "Good idea, yes please."

Nigel walked into the kitchen and Libby heard the cork being withdrawn from another bottle of Rioja. "Have you any peanuts?" he called.

"Yes, in the cupboard to the left of the microwave," she answered.

Nigel walked back to where Libby was sitting and placed a brimming wine glass into her hand. "Sorry, I've filled it a bit too much. Take a big mouthful before you spill it. That's my girl, cheers!"

The Rioja was lovely, with the distinct characteristic made by oak-aging. Nigel may have had many faults, but he certainly never chose a bad wine, Libby thought. She took another long sip, preparing to make good her resolution.

She turned to face him. "Nigel, I must talk to you. Please listen to what I have to say—"

He held up a hand to prevent her going on. "Libby, I *know* what you're going to say. I must apologise for my behaviour of late. I have no excuse, except things have been on my mind, and what with work getting in the way, I know I've neglected you abysmally. I promise I'll make it up to you, my darling. Wait until we're together, then you'll see how wonderful it's going to be. You are going to be my perfect woman. By the way, I never did see you in that dress I bought you. You remember the beautiful purple one with the button-down sleeves. You'll look stunning in that. Would you like to try it on now and give me a showing?"

Libby didn't quite know how she held the neutral look on her face. That awful dress! She wished she had given it to the charity shop when she had the chance. "Not now Nigel, I really don't feel like putting on a long-sleeved dress. It's far too hot. What I was going to say was about moving in with you, I'm —"

"Have some more wine, my sweet, here," he said, producing the wine bottle from the coffee table in front of them and hastily refilling her glass. "It's far too good to waste."

Libby watched the rich red wine being poured and again drank deeply, watching Nigel over the rim of her glass. *If only he would let her get a word in! She had never appreciated before how much of a power freak he was. This had better be her last glass or she would be sloshed before she knew it. Already she felt a little tipsy.*

"I also realised I was shockingly rude when I suggested you didn't need any of your things and to move in with just your clothes. Of course you must sort through your belongings and bring your treasures. We'll find room for them somewhere. Come on, drink up, I have something else I want to show you."

Libby sat forward on the sofa, struggling to interrupt Nigel. He was being very tiresome, plying her with wine and cutting in whenever she had something to say. She had to get him to shut up and understand! As she sat up, the room suddenly seemed to move and things went out of focus. Her eyes gaped at the curtains drawn across the French windows. Was she imagining it?

"Nigel, I feel—"

"What's that, my love? Do you feel all right? Drink your wine. It'll make you feel better."

Libby was aware of his nearness as he held the glass to her lips and helped her to gulp it down. There was a whooshing noise in her ears, and she was finding it difficult to hold her head up. "I feel odd. I can't keep my head—"

All she could see was Nigel's grinning face before her as he poured the wine down her throat and then tossed the glass down onto to the table. Libby watched as if in slow motion as the glass toppled over and broke on the wooden table top. Slivers of jagged glass fell onto the floor below.

"Now, my love, I have your first surprise here for you," he whispered, drawing a package from his jacket pocket. Libby watched helplessly as he undid the jeweller's box and slid a silver bracelet from the black velvet into his hand. "This is for you, my darling. I've had this for some time, and I've been waiting for the right moment to give it to you. Isn't it beautiful? I've found the perfect gift for one as precious as you. Now we've agreed when you're to move in, I think this the ideal time."

"But I'm not—" Powerless and speechless, Libby lay on the sofa as he brushed her skirt above her knees and fixed the bracelet around her ankle. Once in place he sat back to admire his handiwork, a smile on his face. Libby could feel her eyelids drooping, heavy as lead.

"Voila! And now, my darling girl, I believe we need to celebrate in style. I want to show you how much." His eyes glittered strangely as he scooped her unresisting body up into his arms and carried her into her bedroom. A startled, pale ginger cat flew from the bed and shot out of the door, its hair standing up in spikes and uttering a meow of alarm as Nigel aimed a kick at its departing body. The cat tore down the hall towards the kitchen and hid behind the door.

Libby vaguely realised where she was as Nigel began to slowly undress her, savouring every part of her body that he uncovered. She made one last attempt to make a protest before a penetrating blackness descended on her. Through the darkness, she felt a sharp pain tearing deep within her, and she unwillingly uttered a cry as Nigel entered her savagely. As she felt panic engulfing her, Libby mercifully fell into a deep oblivion of total blackness.

Chapter 40

Jem was half way through his shift when he espied the two policemen entering the emergency room. Despite being in plain clothes, Jem knew a policeman when he saw one. A young student nurse turned her startled eyes towards him as she directed the two officers over towards the nurses' station.

"Mr Brookes, sir?"

"Yes that's me. How can I help you, Officers?"

"Do you know a Mr Foster? Peter Foster?"

"Indeed I do. He's a porter here."

"Is there anywhere we might have a few words in private, sir?"

Jem indicated the office half way down the corridor and shooed an inquisitive staff nurse from the room. "Please sit down," he said, wondering what all this was about. The older policeman informed Jem he was a detective inspector. He sat forward in his chair, while the younger constable took out a notebook and pencil. He licked the tip of the graphite while waiting to take notes.

"So, what's Peter done?" Jem asked, thinking how on earth someone as benign and placid as Peter could have got himself into trouble. "Don't tell me he's finally nicked a train up in London. He's fascinated by all those engines, you know."

The inspector sat up in his chair. "When was the last time you saw Mr Foster, Mr Brookes?"

Surprised, Jem looked from one policeman to the other. "Yesterday evening, why?"

"Where was that, sir?"

"We met at the pub. You know the one, The Jolly Sailor, down at Hamble village. We stayed chatting for a while, and then he left. We were supposed to be meeting a friend of mine, but he couldn't make it."

"And what time would this be?"

"Well, we were there quite late. I suppose Peter left just before last orders. I remember wondering why he left before finishing his pint. It was rather sudden. Anyway, I wandered up to the bar and ordered another pint and the barman told me to—"

"Yes sir?" The constable looked up, a quizzical look on his face.

Jem wondered if he should let on about the time as he didn't want to get the bar staff in trouble. "Well, actually it was over time, but the bar man let me have another as long as I drank it quick. They'd been pretty quiet all evening, and I guess the takings were low."

"I see. Go on."

"Well, there's nothing much else to say. We met, had a chat, and Peter left just before closing time. I was about ten or fifteen minutes after."

"Did you speak to anyone else in the pub? Do you go there regularly?"

"Pretty regularly, a few times a month I suppose, especially if I've been out sailing on someone's boat. I don't know about anyone else in the pub. I might have said 'hello' to one or two that I recognised. Can you please tell me what this is all about? What's Peter done?"

When the two policemen looked from one to the other, Jem felt a shock pass through him.

"Is he all right?"

"I'm sorry, sir, but we have to inform you that Mr Foster is dead."

Jem felt the blood drain from his face at the policeman's words. Shocked, he looked from one to the other. "Dead? How? When? Oh my God!"

"Mr Foster was found late this morning. His body was discovered by a walker and his dog on the lower shores of Warsash, near where the River Hamble enters the Solent. We need to establish where he was before he entered the water. We believe you might be the last person to have seen him alive."

"Well, it was high tide at about eleven last night. If he fell in after leaving the pub, then the current must have carried him down the river. On the shore you say?" Jem found his heart was pounding with the appalling news. Peter dead!

"Yes, the marshy bit past where the ferry is."

"I suppose it's possible he fell in near the marina. But why he was near the water, I can't say."

"Can you tell us what sort of mood he was in last night? Had he had much to drink? We'll be checking with the pub later, of course."

"Yes, of course. Well no, he only had part of his pint, as I said earlier. Mood? He seemed a bit nervous, agitated almost. Look, I don't know what you've been told about Peter, but he was a nice guy; quiet and respectable and kept himself to himself. He actually suffered from Asperger's Syndrome and preferred his own company. He was an enthusiastic railway buff, and the only other hobby of his was stage make-up. He belonged to a local amateur drama group."

"Which one, sir?"

"Sorry, I don't know. I think I'd better tell you why we met last night." Jem looked towards the office door to check that it was closed.

The two officers exchanged glances again and the constable shuffled in his seat as he leaned forward to catch Jem's words.

"It's to do with the attacks on the nurses here. Peter reckoned that he might have seen someone acting suspiciously when the second nurse was attacked."

The two policemen raised their eyebrows with interest. "Go on."

"I think it was just a hunch, but he seemed quite positive at the time. Apparently, Peter called back into work that evening, something about picking up a magazine he'd left behind. He knows all the shortcuts around the place, and he noticed this guy, a doctor, hanging around an area that's usually deserted at that time of night. Peter has an uncanny habit of remembering almost everything in minute detail, and he said this doctor was actually wearing a wig and stage make-up. But good stage make-up, he said. He indicated that the guy knew what he was doing when he made his face up."

"Interesting, and did he say what this 'doctor' looked like? Any distinguishing features?"

"Nothing more than the nurse has already given you: short dark hair and a thin body of medium height. No, the point I'm making – in fact what Peter was making – is that the attacker was definitely disguising his face."

"I see. Anything else?"

"Yes." Jem looked troubled before carrying on with his explanation. "Peter said he was worried that the attacker was targeting nurses who were blonde."

"How did he make that assumption then?"

"I'm not sure." Jem paused and then sighed. "Look, if you must know, there's a sister here who Peter reckoned looks a bit like the nurse who was attacked. Peter, being as he is – was – took it into his head to go and visit this sister with the thought of warning her. The sister, who's called Libby, caught him loitering outside her house, and she was a bit startled. A mutual friend suggested he and I should speak to Peter, quiet like, and ask him what he thought he was doing. That's all."

"And this mutual friend, what's his name then?"

"Robert. He's the other friend who was supposed to meet me and Peter in the pub."

"Aha. So Mr Foster, Peter, was nervous because of what he'd been doing? Stalking this Sister Libby or whatever her name is."

Jem thought for a moment. Was that right? "I'm not sure," he said, pausing as that evening in the pub went through his mind. "He was a bit agitated at first, and then he seemed to settle down. We were chatting, and then he suddenly stopped. He was looking out of the pub window one minute, then stopped what he was saying and announced that he had to be somewhere else and couldn't wait to meet Robert."

"So did he know Robert or not?"

"No."

"And it was this Robert who failed to turn up. Do you know why?"

"No, I'm sorry. He telephoned me a few minutes after Peter had left to say he'd been held up somewhere."

"This gets more and more interesting. I think we need to get in touch with Robert. Do you have a contact number?"

Jem looked troubled as he got out his mobile and searched the address book for the number. Something wasn't right, and he didn't just mean Peter's death. He felt that this was going to be a very long day, and by the look of things, the police hadn't finished with him yet.

Chapter 41

Taking advantage of her daughter's nap, Diana was relaxing in Robert's garden with a cup of tea and idling with pad and pencil. Ten months had elapsed since she had finished writing her last book, *Children of the Plantation,* and for the first time since then, she felt the urge to write another novel.

It the truth be known, she was feeling a bit puzzled over her cousin's behaviour. She knew Robert had been devastated when Morwenna and baby Carole were found dead at the bottom of the cliff, and it had taken years before he could bring himself to talk about it. Ever since she had been staying with him, she was pleased to find he was coping and finally coming to terms with his loss. The arrival of Libby on the scene seemed to have fanned the fires towards the possibility of a romance too.

So why wasn't Robert making the most of it? Diana already knew from what she had been told that Libby was going to ditch her fiancé surgeon. When Robert talked about her, his fascination was obvious, but still he dithered.

That wasn't all. The whole scenario seemed odd. Diana swiftly went through the chain of events; there was an attacker at Southampton General with a 'liking' for blonde nurses; Libby had been the subject of an intruder, who had wandered around her home for some apparent reason, and as a result, Robert had checked all her doors and windows making sure they were secure; Libby was attached to this surgeon, whose ex-wife seemed to stay for unhealthy lengths of time with him, making Robert suspect there was still something between them. Diana agreed with him over this. It was obvious, surely.

Then there was the hospital porter, Peter. Although Robert and Libby's friend Jem said he was an 'okay' guy, he supposedly thought he had seen the hospital stalker during one night of an attack, and he had positioned himself at Libby's house one day causing her a fright if nothing else. Now, according to the news and Robert's own terse account, this Peter had been found dead. Moreover, he was found dead after his meeting with Jem *and* Robert was supposed to have been at that meeting.

What a mixed bag of events. As she thought more and more, Diana realised that everything was surely connected. Was Peter killed, or was his death an accident? Nothing had been disclosed by the police yet.

Sitting in the afternoon sun letting her mind wander freely over the recent happenings, Diana had another thought. If Peter had seen the attacker, then he may have been killed to keep him quiet. The attacker had suddenly become a murderer.

As the sun disappeared behind a stray cloud, Diana felt a chill and gave a shudder. She was sure she was right. There was something else that was niggling away at the back of her mind, which she couldn't put her finger on. It just wouldn't come. She gave a sigh. Maybe she would work it out later that day.

Diana heard movement in the house, and when she turned round, she saw Robert walking out to join her in the garden. He looked tired and strained, she thought, as he gave her a thin smile and sat down on the grass. She pondered over what he had told her when they had shared cocoa together. Robert hadn't spoken to Peter that evening in the pub as he had been detained at the base. If so, why had his jeans been wet at the bottom?

"Any more news?" she asked, watching her clearly troubled cousin as he lay down at her feet. He put his hands behind his head and crossed his ankles in an effort to appear relaxed.

"Jem says the police are definitely treating Peter's death as suspicious. The autopsy will prove whether there was water in his lungs or not. If there was, I suppose he was killed before he entered the water."

Diana agreed, nodding. "That's usual." She let the silence between them grow as she finished her tea.

"I've just had an idea come to me."

"What's that then?" Robert swivelled his head round, squinting at her.

"Something's been niggling me for some time. You told me Peter was a train fanatic as well as being pretty good with stage make-up."

"Yes, so what?"

"Have you realised that the nurses at St Thomas's Hospital in London have also been stalked and attacked over the past few weeks?"

"Ye–es. What's your point?"

"Well, my point is, could they be connected? Or is it pure coincidence or even a copycat at work?"

"I get you. It's possible I suppose – good grief! Are you suggesting Peter was the attacker all along? That he attacked nurses at both hospitals? That's a bit far-fetched isn't it?" Robert sat up, a look of horror on his face

"Probably, but all the same, he used to visit the London train stations to watch out for particular engines. St Thomas's is not that far from Waterloo. He could easily kill two birds with one stone: visit the station and the hospital. He's also good with make-up. Just a thought."

"Except he's now dead."

"Yes, and it all depends on whether he was murdered or had an accident. Or, there again, he could have committed suicide, I suppose."

"I don't know, Di. An awful lot of people must commute between the two cities. There's Libby's lover or ex-lover for instance. He works here and in London, according to Libby. Wait a minute. He did lose his mobile at the time of one of the attacks. Now there's a coincidence!"

Diana laughed. "I'm sorry, this is serious. It's just that you're so transparent over your feelings towards Libby's fiancé. Why don't you admit you're in love with her?"

"I'm…not. And yes, Nigel is a complete and utter prick as far as I'm concerned. He has treated Libby so badly lately, ignoring her and then snapping his fingers when it suits him."

"Pooh, I don't believe you, and as for Nigel being a prick, so he might be, but there's no reason to believe he has anything to do with this."

The silence settled on them like a cape while they were lost in their thoughts.

"You sure?"

"Robert, nothing is sure until proven, but your theory is a long shot. No, I think the clue is in the stage make-up. The attacker didn't want to be recognised. So the person must be local and well-known."

Robert shifted his body on the grass. "I think I'll go in. The grass is getting damp. Would you like more tea?"

"Yes please. I must wake Poppy, or she'll never sleep tonight. I can't wait for Steve to join us next week. By the way, have you spoken to Libby today?"

"No, not yet. She didn't tell me what hours she was working today, but she's bound to be there now. I'll make the tea, and then give her a ring."

Chapter 42

It was inconvenient, but it had to be done. The porter had seen the face of the attacker, albeit under stage make-up. There was something in his eyes, a look that told the attacker to be very, very aware. It would be unforgiveable to be identified now.

The game was nearly over. It was too bad that the final scene was to be played away from the water. That really was the attacker's favourite place. No matter; in less than an hour it would all be concluded.

She would be mine to do with as I please, no one else's, and that is what surely mattered.

Chapter 43

Libby was barely awake as she stumbled from her bed. Her bladder felt as if it was bursting, and she wondered why her body ached so much as she staggered to the bathroom. Standing in front of the mirror, she was horrified to see bruises around her mouth and neck. As she examined them closer, it looked as if she had been subjected to a series of bites from a small dog. What on earth had happened to her? She tried to clear her muzzy head and think back to her last unobstructed recollections. There was nothing there!

Almost sobbing in terror, she teetered back to her bedroom and surveyed the scene before her eyes. Her bed was a complete mess with the covers hanging off, and as her vision cleared, she saw what looked like small spatters of blood covering the bottom sheet. What had happened?

Think! Think! She told herself. What can you remember last? She glanced over at her bedside clock and saw that it was early morning. The fog began to lift from her eyes as she noticed the silver bracelet and suddenly thought of Nigel. What had they done? What had he done to her, she corrected herself, wincing at the pain between her thighs.

He had called round last evening sometime around nine o'clock. They had been very civil and enjoyed a few glasses of wine, red wine, maybe even Rioja? Libby recalled Nigel slipping the bracelet on her ankle and running his fingers over her legs, kissing her neck, and then she couldn't remember any more until she woke up just a few minutes ago.

She ran her hands over her body, flinching as she felt more welts upon her breasts and stomach. As she slowly realised what had happened, tears fell from her eyes. Soon she was sobbing, curled up in a small ball after discovering the evil her so-called fiancé had done to her.

~~~~~

How long she lay there, she couldn't remember, but once she stopped crying the pain became more intense. The only thing she could think of, to ease her body and rid her of the humiliation, was to soak in a deep bath. Once she slipped into the silky water, she felt the dirt and shame begin to leave her. She scrubbed her hair and body, cringing, but never baulking as she endeavoured to wash away her degradation.

When she had finished, she felt a little better, and her embarrassment turned to anger. How could he? How on earth did he manage to trick her? As she replayed the previous evening's events over and over in her mind, she realised Nigel must have spiked her drink. But why? It was true they hadn't slept with one another since her return from hospital, but was he so depraved that he needed to possess her no matter what? Her thoughts turned back to one other occasion on his yacht. Hadn't she woken then, confused and feeling out of sorts with vague aches over her body?

The pig! The absolute bastard! Well, he wasn't going to get away scot-free this time. She would get even somehow.

~~~~~

Libby decided she needed a course of action. She had taken a bath and so washed away any traces of him on her. She didn't know for certain how long a date-rape drug like Rohypnol stayed in the body, but she was pretty sure it was as long as 60 hours. Certainly long enough for her to telephone the police and get a blood sample taken. As she considered her choices, the tears began to fall once again. Never had she felt so miserable. If only someone dependable like Robert was here.

It was late morning when Libby finally roused herself. After her fresh bout of tears, she had fallen into a deep sleep. She put on a light dress and wandered through to the kitchen. Rommie greeted her with a loud purr as Libby opened a tin of cat food, enjoying the simple acts of stroking and having the cat rub herself around her legs. She felt the telltale pricking of tears once more and gave herself a scolding. Self-pity would not do!

Selecting a high-strength coffee capsule, Libby switched the coffee machine on. A strong brew was just what she needed. Food was out of the question, so she carried her steaming cup through to her living room and sat down on the sofa. She noticed a broken wine glass that had toppled over and a dried splash of red wine on the oak coffee table. Beneath the table, there were the slivers of glass shards from the broken glass. Libby tried to remember if she had broken it and when, but she couldn't recall the episode. She picked up the pieces of loose glass in her hand and was about to take them into the kitchen for disposal when there was a distinct noise from her hallway. Slowly, with the hairs beginning to stand up on the back of her neck, Libby turned her head towards the sound. There in the doorway stood a figure dressed in a doctor's white coat: medium height, slim body, dark short hair.

Libby stood up and, with a cry of astonishment, shouted, "Who the hell are you? How did you get in?"

The doctor smiled and raised a hand displaying Libby's front door key. "You were careless, dearest Libby. It was a simple thing to have another one cut."

As Libby began to move away from the sofa, the stranger hissed at her to remain where she was. It was then Libby saw the long blade in the other hand. Panic gripped her, and she felt as if her feet were bolted to the floor. As the intruder moved towards Libby, she saw her chance. Libby bent down and with one hand shoved the end of the coffee table at the intruder's knees and then darted towards the kitchen. She knew she would never make it to the front door. If only she could escape through the kitchen, she could run into the garden and scream as loudly as possible. She heard a loud oath behind her as the heavy table was thrust away. Libby reached the door, dropped the broken glass pieces onto the floor, and wrestled with the lock...the one Robert had fitted. As she tried to turn and release the safety catch, she heard her assailant behind her. Sobs escaped Libby as she struggled in vain. The lock would not budge. Libby spun round to fend off her attacker and felt the blow from a vase as it smashed into the side of her head.

Chapter 44

Just as planned, the attacker would follow the same procedure with Libby as with her other four sisters in death; with legs bound together and her arms pinned to her sides with strong gaffer tape. When Libby woke up and realised what was happening, despite being able to squirm around a bit, she wouldn't be able to move enough to save herself.

More tape was twisted around the limp body. When she did awaken, she would be told precisely what and why it was all happening. The others had experienced the exact same procedure, and although a marine environment would have been ideal, Libby's flat would suffice. This was the last time, after all, and Libby deserved to be informed of how she was a vital part in the ritual.

She could have been killed from the vicious blow to her head, but that hadn't been in the plan. The vase was only meant to stun her, to make her weak and pliable, as helpless as a kitten while she was bound. The attacker stood back as Libby began to stir and waited until she was alert enough to take in what she was about to be told.

"You have to understand, Libby," she began, her voice sounding reasonable and calm, "you got far too close for comfort. I would never have planned any of this if he hadn't kept going on and on about how well-suited you both were. Normally, after a few weeks, he would have tired of you and returned home to me. Now, *we* are well-matched. You shouldn't have listened to his old, often-told story about how you were the one and how wonderful you and he being together was all going to be. I've heard it all a hundred times before."

She checked the tape around Libby's arms and legs. She was lying on the floor in front of the kitchen door. The back garden was secluded and the attacker didn't have to worry about being overlooked by neighbours.

"I've always viewed his affairs with interest and often admired how he managed to play one woman off against another. But with you, it was different. He said he didn't need me anymore, and I would be in the way. Me! The one who helped keep him supplied with Temazepam to make his victims soft and easy targets. It's funny how he loves using drugs like that, but I understand it's a complete power thing with Nigel. It didn't take me long to analyse him of course. Once he began experimenting on his clinic cases, I could see where all this was leading. He nearly got caught once when an irate husband suspected his shoddy little tricks, but Nigel had good counsel and is renowned for his smooth talking." She smiled as she paused and sat back on her heels running a hand over Libby's bonds.

"It's been amusing over the years, but sometimes he forgot our pact, like with you. Like with Amy. She's been dead three years. Her body's lying somewhere on the bed of the River Thames, weighted down with stones. Amy loved London and thought she would make Nigel a marvellous wife. Or fair Elizabeth, whose bones are rotting in the ancient woodland of Hampstead Heath; with Gemma, whom I left forever sleeping in a blanket of leaves in the New Forest just west of Southampton; and finally, dear little blonde Susan slumbering deeply in the salt-marsh thick reeds of the shores of Dibden Bay. Did you realise Nigel has a fixation for pretty blonde women? Always nurses, of course. Yes, you my dear will be joining all these women – your sisters in death. Did you ever wonder about those other nurses? The pretty blonde ones who were stalked and attacked at night? Those were just *pure fun*. I loved to see their faces change from their ridiculous looks that spoke of their feeling of being above any danger. It was all so easy to lull them into a deep sense of false security when I chatted to them. You should have seen their smug faces transform once they saw my blade! I never wanted to kill any of them. It was enough to mess with them just a little, rearrange their looks. They were women of a certain ilk."

She added another strand of tape around Libby's hands, as if in anger as she recalled her gruesome activities. She stayed bent over Libby, her voice low and calm, almost conversational as she reminisced. "Why the disguise, you're probably thinking. Well, I was too well-known among the hospital staff both here and in London. Oh yes, all the girls in London were my own little ventures, and it was almost too easy applying make-up and a dark wig. You see, I'm another of Nigel's blonde girls too, except I'm not like you or them. I'm in charge. I control everything."

~~~~~

Through the mist in her brain, Libby was aware of a voice just above her head. She was sure she had heard the voice before…somewhere…but her head felt as if it was on fire with pain, and she didn't dare open her eyes. Struggling to pull herself together, she wondered, what is happening to me? I know that voice from sometime back. Libby had a flash of memory. She recalled a doctor standing just inside the entrance to her living room. It was strange though. Why would he be wearing a coat here? In fact why was he here at all? She thought some more, beginning to focus better. Wait! That was a woman's voice. So were there two people here?

Libby opened her eyes.

It wasn't a male doctor at all. The face, only inches away from her, was a woman's. As her mind finally cleared, she recognised her. Her eyes glittered, shining with the kind of madness Libby had seen in the eyes of only a few patients during her nursing career. Only, those patients had been locked away. She's mad! It was Stella! Stella dressed in a doctor's coat and without the dark wig, recognisable with her longer blonde tresses. Libby knew her from those lectures long ago when she had worked in London. She stared into

Stella's eyes, which was like looking into bowls of pale blue ice.

"Everything is ready for you, Libby. See, I have your shroud here." She gave a sudden laugh. "Do you remember that old novel of P D James? 'A Shroud for a Nightingale'. How apt! I've just realised how fitting this all is. You will be wearing the same as the others. Those who thought they could step into my shoes."

Stella stood up, and Libby could see she was holding a large plastic bag in front of her. It was a bag big enough to completely cover her small body. Libby bit back a sob. Oh please God, no! she thought. Please don't let her suffocate me!

"This is my favourite part of the game, Libby, so I'll do it nice and slow. That way I can watch your face. I really enjoy watching. You'll know when the air runs out, when you gasp for breath. I'll just take it slowly because you'll want to live a little bit longer, won't you? I don't think it'll hurt, and don't worry, I'm not going to cut you. No, I prefer to save my beautiful blade for the also-rans. When you're finally asleep, you'll be as lovely as Nigel remembered you, my dear."

Stella stooped down and positioned the bag over Libby's feet. She paused when she saw the silver bracelet around Libby's slim ankle.

"Funny how he has them engraved, isn't it? And with my own chosen words too! Such a coincidence." She slid the plastic underneath Libby until her feet and legs were completely enclosed. Libby kicked out against the plastic, but her bound legs and feet were useless.

The telephone rang in the other room, and Stella paused to listen.

"Please don't! Stella, you mustn't so this! Nigel means nothing to me. I broke it off the other night, you must believe me. He's all yours! I don't want him," she begged.

Stella stared into her eyes. "Don't play games with me. I've seen you together acting like a tart on his yacht. Oh yes, you're a tart all right. I know all about you and that helicopter pilot. Nigel told me. If Nigel meant nothing to you, why does he have a key to this place?" As she leaned in towards Libby, she caught a whiff of a familiar limey citrus scent.

"It was you that night!" Libby gasped. "You were the intruder!"

"You're catching on fast. Now lie still while I bring your shroud up higher."

The telephone stopped ringing as she pulled the bag up over Libby's hips and waist. Libby struggled, but she was no match for the wiry and strong Stella. As the bag reached Libby's chest and neck, she let out a terrified scream.

Stella paused, placing a finger to her lips. "Hush! No one will hear you scream. Remember this was your destiny from the very first day you went out with Nigel. In doing so, you became mine, all mine."

Libby thought of screaming again, but would anyone hear? She opened her mouth and only stopped when Stella held the knife to her throat.

"Please don't make me do this, Libby. I truly don't want to hurt you. My way is beautiful."

Libby studied her face as Stella poised above her, a distant look in her eyes. Libby gave a sob. She's completely mad and she's going to kill me. She killed all Nigel's other serious girlfriends, and now it's my turn!

Chapter 45

Diana finished feeding Poppy and, after giving her a cuddle, took her upstairs for a bath. She chuckled at the grubby-faced little cherub, blowing raspberries from the tub and swirled a sudsy sponge over the tiny body.

"Come on little one, time for your nap."

Dried and smelling sweetly of baby talc and lotion, the sleepy infant was placed by her mother into the cot. Within seconds she was asleep. There was no need to tiptoe from the room because Poppy was proving to be the perfect baby. Diana could run a vacuum cleaner around the room, but she never woke up until she had had enough rest.

When she went back downstairs, she spied a troubled-looking Robert leaning deep in thought against the wall in the hall.

"What's up?" she asked. "Did you ring Libby?"

"I did. She's not answering at home, so I rang her ward. Lisa, her workmate, said she was due in at lunchtime and hasn't showed yet. She said her mobile was switched off, so she couldn't get hold of her. She sounded concerned as Libby was supposed to let her know how it went with Nigel. Libby told Lisa she was definitely going to chuck him. So where is she? Finally, I rang Jem, who's just had a visit from the police."

Diana thought. "I don't like the sound of any of this."

"Neither do I. Jem says the police are treating Peter's death as very suspicious. Two detectives are on the case apparently, and Jem thinks he was murdered. He reckons that Peter was definitely on to something with the suspicious doctor."

"I think he's right. Originally, we talked vaguely about Peter being the attacker up in London and down here. I personally believe Peter did witness the attacker here, and the clue is in the make-up and disguise. The attacker must have realised Peter saw him on that night and tracked him down. I believe Peter was an innocent victim and the attacker is someone else and yes, the two hospitals are connected."

"That leads us back to my theory about Nigel."

"It does, but I did some research earlier on. Did you know Nigel was almost prosecuted for an alleged misconduct at his London clinic? He was accused by an irate husband of sexually interfering with his wife while under sedation."

"Libby!"

"What about Libby?"

"She said she woke up on Nigel's boat feeling very odd and couldn't remember what had happened. She also said she couldn't remember a lot of things where he was concerned."

"How tall is this Nigel?"

"Hmm, a bit taller than me I think, thinner though. Maybe it isn't him after all."

"The attacker is said to be of medium height and slight build. Mmm, make-up and wig. Do you know what I'm thinking? I'm not sure you'll believe me."

Robert shook his head.

"I believe our attacker isn't Nigel at all."

"No?"

"No. I think we're looking for a woman."

"A woman? Who the devil—"

"Peter said there was something odd about the hospital attacker, which he couldn't put his finger on, didn't he?"

"According to Jem."

"So, unless we have a whole mishmash of unconnected events and someone not connected with any of this, I believe the murderer to be a woman. As Peter said, the make-up wasn't quite right. What if it was a woman dressed up as a man?"

"So which woman?"

"We're looking for someone who knows hospital procedures, dress code, layouts of the grounds etcetera; who regularly travels between Southampton and London and probably needs somewhere to stay in both areas where they can lie low for a while. Nigel is involved somehow, but I'm not sure how, except maybe by his earlier misdemeanour. There's only one person who completely fits the bill."

Diana looked at Robert with an alarmed look on her face.

"His wife!" they chorused.

"I don't like this one bit. I think I'd better get over there at once. See if she's there. You know, she might have a faulty telephone line, and Lisa said she had her mobile turned off."

"How long will it take you?"

"Twenty minutes, if I'm lucky. Ring the police, and let them know what we suspect," he yelled as he ran towards the door, car keys in hand.

"Good luck, and be careful. Don't forget; whoever it is, *is* dangerous."

"So am I, where Libby is concerned," he retorted, throwing open the door.

When he had gone, the telephone rang, and Diana went to answer it. As she picked up the receiver, she had a premonition it would be the police on the other end.

"You've just missed him. I was about to call you. No, he's gone into Southampton to see…yes, that's right, Libby Hunter. No, she lives in Southampton. He might have her current address written down in his address book. Hang on while I get it."

As Diana thumbed through the pages she couldn't help a tremor of dread go through her. She hoped and prayed she was right about this, but above all, she desperately hoped Robert would get there in time.

Chapter 46

Robert drove like a maniac through the back streets of Southampton, avoiding the traffic, speed cameras, and waiting policemen. He wanted to get to Libby's as soon as possible. Deep down, he knew Diana was right. She had this uncanny knack of looking at something from a distance and putting her finger exactly on the spot.

Please let me be in time! He begged silently while sounding his horn at an itinerant jaywalker. He picked up his mobile and dialled her home again. No answer – just as he expected and put his foot down harder on the accelerator.

Chapter 47

"Libby, it won't be long now. The time is right. You'll be snug and comfortable in your shroud."

I have to keep her talking, Libby thought. The phone had rung again, and somehow she knew it was Robert trying to get through to her. Please let him come, she begged silently as tears rolled down her cheeks. Would he sense the danger and terror she was in and come to her rescue? My hero once, would he succeed again? She sobbed uncontrollably as panic took over.

Stella paused as she stroked Libby's throat. "Too bad you were the prettiest. But no matter, now I can have Nigel all to myself once again."

"Stella," she said, trying to control the quiver in her voice. "Please think. This is not going to do you or Nigel any good. My friends know all about this. I'm sure they've told the police by now. They'll put all the facts together and guess what's happened."

"It won't work, Libby. You're too late. You should have thought of the consequences before you stole Nigel" Stella murmured.

I have to get through to her. She's an intelligent woman – a psychiatrist! "Stella, how will Nigel feel once he finds out? Will he want you then?"

"Don't try the psychology with me. Remember who *I* am! Nigel will do as he's told, as he's done for years. You won't know this, but he's actually *enjoyed* our little games. I know this is the last, and that's okay because we can get back to where we were before," she said in a dismissive tone.

Stella began to play with the bag. Very slowly, she drew up the zipper until it covered half of Libby's face.

"Stella, you need help. You won't get away with this. What will Nigel do then, if you're locked away?" Libby pleaded.

"But I want to do this, Libby. You are the final one in my mission. Lie still, and be a good girl. The time is now."

Stella took hold of the bag, and in one single movement, pulled it the rest of the way over Libby's head. She took hold of the zipper and velcroed ends and sealed the bag's opening. After a long last look at Libby's shrouded body, she stood up. "It will only take about ten minutes, Libby. Sleep in peace."

Chapter 48

As soon as Libby heard Stella walking away, she began to struggle. She knew the air wouldn't last long in the bag. If she could only keep her head and not panic, short and shallow breaths would mean the oxygen would last longer. Within minutes, she began to feel lightheaded.

All her nursing training screamed at her to keep cool, while her lungs screamed for air! As she fought to keep in control, her chest began to hurt, and she realised she might pass out. She was finding it hard to breathe, and her mind was playing weird tricks.

Robert would come. He *had* to! Surely he wouldn't let her down. I don't want to die. I don't want to die, especially now I've met Robert. The words were screaming through her head as she struggled to survive.

She could feel the rigid cold surface of the kitchen floor beneath her body through the plastic bag. With as much concentration as she could muster, she kicked hard against the bag and thought she felt one foot protrude through the plastic hitting the door beyond. The floor felt hard against her body, with small bumps here and there beneath her back.

Somewhere, a thought wormed its way uppermost in her brain, something to do with the door and glass. The glass of the kitchen door was double-glazed and almost impossible to break – but wait! Libby recalled the broken wine glass she had dropped when she had tried to open the kitchen door. Gasping for breath and with the plastic bag sticking to her face and throat, Libby wriggled her body over the lumps beneath her. In desperation she ground her body down upon the bumps, blackness enveloping her.

She frantically moved her body back and forth. A sudden, sharp pain hit her as the slivers of glass sliced through the plastic, through her clothing and into her skin. Dimly, she could feel blood seeping from her wounds as the plastic began to give way. Sobbing for air, she kept moving, the pain from the glass keeping her mind alive. As the blood gushed from her wounds, she thought she felt a hint of fresh air.

Twenty minutes later, Robert kicked in the front door and found her lying in a pool of blood. Libby! With trembling hands he tore off the plastic bag and felt for her heart beat. She was alive!

Chapter 49

Libby opened her eyes and studied the figure sitting beside her bed. She stiffened, instantly reminded of another such incident, one which seemed so long ago. So much had happened since then. She felt sore and bruised along her back and legs, and as she felt beneath the bed covers, she couldn't quite stifle a groan.

"Libby. How are you feeling?"

"Sore. Groggy."

"I'm not surprised you've a huge swelling on your head and about twenty stitches in your back." He moved nearer to look at her face in the dimmed light. She looked exhausted, with deep dark shadows circling her eyes.

"Do I look as bad as I feel?" she whispered.

"You look beautiful," he said, curling his fingers around hers.

"Did you catch her?" She attempted to sit up as she suddenly remembered her last moments of terror.

"Sssh. It's all over. Yes, we did. Diana filled the police in with our suspicions, well Di's suspicions really, and they arrested both Stella and Nigel."

"Nigel too?" she enquired softly.

"Yes, of course. For his part in drugging you, and for knowing deep down just what Stella had been doing all these years."

Libby lay back relieved and visibly relaxed. She closed her eyes as tears threatened to escape. The past few hours had been so traumatic. Robert put his arms around her and held her close.

"Please don't—" she said.

Alarmed Robert drew back. "Don't what?"

"Please don't ever stop holding me."

Robert stared down into her tear-laden eyes. "Never my love, never ever."

~~~~~

Sometime later there was a knock on the door, and Robert stood up to admit Diana. She softly enquired whether she might come in when Libby turned to see who her new visitor was.

"I think it is about time you two met," Robert said as Diana approached the bed.

"I'm sure we're going to be good friends," Diana said, smiling at Libby. "Robert has told me all about you. I think you're exactly what he needs."

The two women eyed each other as Robert held his breath. Apart from his sister, they were the two most important females in his life, and it was imperative that they got along.

Libby returned Diana's smile. "I did wonder at first if I might have a rival. That was until Robert explained about you."

Robert let out his breath in relief. Things were going to be okay. A noise at the half-closed door had them looking towards the disturbance.

"Steve!"

"I thought I might find you all here. Wherever there's trouble, you can count on Diana being in the thick of it. How are you, my darling? Are you going to tell me what you've been up to this time?"

Robert laughed at the guilty look on his cousin's face as she gazed lovingly at her husband. "Don't worry about her, Steve. It looks like we have someone else who's just as accident-prone, trouble following wherever she goes. Sit down, and we'll fill you in. You have no idea what you've missed."

Faith Mortimer

The Surgeon's Blade – Faith Mortimer

January 2012

Excerpt from "Children of the Plantation"
by Faith Mortimer

"Children of the Plantation" by Faith Mortimer.

Prologue

Opening the kitchen door, Hermione spotted a vixen standing near the refuse bin. She clapped her hands, and it shot through the hedge at the bottom of the garden.

Hermione's heart was thudding in her breast as she considered what next to do. Casting a look around, she gave thanks that the clouds scudding overhead made it a dark night. This had to be done in complete privacy.

Giving herself a mental shake, she crossed the damp grass to the shed and picked up a spade. A clod of earth still clung to the sharp blade from where she had been digging in her vegetable patch earlier that afternoon. It seemed such a long time ago now. She paused, still not completely certain she was doing the right thing. Making up her mind, she walked over to the newly turned earth.

The air smelt fresh after the rain shower, and a light breeze blew the mixed garden scents her way while she dug. The hole was to be small but deep, especially as she had just driven the fox off. Satisfied, she stood back and peered down into the soft loamy material, a sorry place for such a pathetic bundle.

Sick at heart, but knowing they had no choice, Hermione laid down her spade and walked back into the kitchen. She picked up the tightly wrapped package and carried it outside; it weighed no more than a couple of pounds as she gently laid it down into the hole.

Covering it with fresh earth, she scattered pebbles around and knelt on the grass. Had there been any other choice? Whatever were they going to tell him when the time came?

Chapter 1

October 2011

High above Kuala Lumpur's international airport, the Emirates airbus began to make its controlled descent.

From her window seat, Diana had a marvellous view of the capital of Malaysia. She had supposed they would be looking down upon a sea of luxuriant vegetation, jungle and scrub, but the serried rank and file below suggested organised plantations rather than virgin wilderness.

"Well, Mrs Rivers. What can you see?" Steve asked, leaning towards her from the adjacent seat. "Can you see the tall towers of KL yet?"

"Mmm. We're circling now. It's a much bigger city than I remember and more modern. When I was last here, there was only a handful of skyscrapers. I suppose this is progress." She sounded disappointed.

Steve gave a chuckle. "You're getting older. You have to remember nothing stays the same for ever. Practically every country in the world wants to improve itself and if that means modernising its towns and cities, it will. The west has used more of the world's resources than the rest of the world put together; you know that."

"I do, but it doesn't necessarily mean it's better or that I have to like it. I wanted Malaya to be how I remembered it when I was young."

"Stop grumbling. Your trouble is you're tired from a long flight. How do you feel, darling?"

Diana smiled at her husband. "Sorry, you're right of course. I am tired and I feel *et-see ket-see* (so-so) as we say at home. My ankles have swollen. I have never had that happen before! I'll be glad when we're finally on the ground."

"Not long now. Look! We're lining up with the runway. This is fun watching our landing on the screen." Steve indicated the overhead monitor showing a frontal camera view. The runway stretched directly ahead. "We'll soon be in the hotel and you can put your feet up. You mustn't overdo it, despite the doctor saying you're fine."

Diana nodded and smiled, thinking back to her last antenatal visit. Thankfully, as everything was in order, her doctor and midwife had agreed she was fit enough to fly long-distance to the Far East for an exotic holiday. As she was healthy and so long as she followed their instructions, she should have no worries. This baby was their first, so both parents were excited and looking forward to completing their family.

The trip to Malaysia was a new experience for Steve, Diana having lived here during part of her childhood. She carried treasured memories of those years and planned to rediscover some of her old haunts, if possible. Looking at the vast and so far unrecognisable city below, she realised that it might prove difficult.

"I can't wait to see the hotel. The brochure description sounds wonderful. '*An old colonial ex-family home, set on a hill surrounded by a plantation of rubber trees, fruit and natural vegetation*' she had read to Steve earlier that week. "I wonder if the countryside is much as I remember."

"I expect there'll be lots of changes, so don't get too excited. Look at the UK now. The rural areas are mostly small pockets dotted between the sprawl of towns and farmland. There's not a lot of true wilderness left anywhere."

Diana knew he was right. Progress again, she decided. Malaysia was supposed to have some proper nature reserves, and she hoped they hadn't cut all of the indigenous trees down and sold the wood to Japan.

~~~~~

The airport was about thirty miles from the city, and Diana and Steve's hotel was further up country. Collecting their luggage from the carousel, they were soon on their way along a fine modern road towards their destination. The road was new tarmacadam and not one of the red-dust tracks Di remembered so well from when she was twelve. One remarkable advance she observed was the fierce air conditioning in the taxi-cab. With the outside temperature and humidity high in the nineties, she soon forgot her misgivings about modern progress.

Forty minutes later, they were bumping along a smaller road, an avenue of trees shading them from the glaring sun. Further from the highway, more and more of the vegetation became wild; Nipa and Nibong palms, epiphytes such as orchids and ferns, bamboos, bananas, and creepers with brilliant flowers of every hue were draped over fences and clambered up the trees, all jostling for space.

"This is more like it," Di said, looking eagerly about. "Much more the Malaysia I knew."

She fell silent as the car pulled off the road through a pair of stately gates hanging from huge square pillars and swept up the driveway. Ahead, she could see an imposing building. Painted white, it was two stories high with a wide, shady veranda which seemed to run completely around the perimeter. The gardens were a riot of colour, numerous varieties of plants competing in the well-tended flower beds. Di caught a glimpse of a small flock of jewel-coloured birds as they flew from what she remembered as a Rambutan fruit tree. Further across the lawns was the welcome glint of blue water coming from a swimming pool.

The whole effect was stunning. Di and Steve looked at each other with delight. This was going to be a perfect place for a relaxing holiday.

~~~~~

Each guest room was a suite comprising a large bedroom complete with a huge en-suite bathroom and a connecting door leading to a comfortable sitting-room. From here, a deep balcony ran along the outer walls of both bedroom and sitting-room. The whole suite was light and airy, the furniture covered in a restful green material with matching drapes and bed cover. Air conditioning and overhead ceiling fans completed the luxury.

Steve soon spied the minibar and declared himself satisfied with the contents. "Everything we need, darling. Plenty of orange juice for you too. Would you like a drink now?"

Di was gazing out of the window at a large flock of brightly-coloured birds. Some with tail-feathers which were remarkably long, while others were dazzling in other ways: pigeons with emerald-coloured wings and others a riot of scarlet. "What I'd really like is a good cup of Malayan-grown tea."

"Good idea. Would you like room service or shall we go down to the lounge?"

"Let's go down. If I stay here, I'll fall asleep on this cosy-looking bed, and I really want to get used to this time zone as soon as possible."

"Are you sure you don't need a rest? You look a bit peaky still."

"Steve I'm fine! I'm pregnant, not ill! Besides, I've been resting for the last God knows how many hours on that plane. Let's go and explore. We might meet some of the other guests. You never know who might be staying here."

Sliding her feet back into her sandals, she rose from her armchair and gave him a big smile. "This place definitely has the look of a Somerset Maugham play, don't you think?" she said, mimicking a perfect upper-class accent. "I wonder if there's an exciting history connected to it."

Matching her accent, Steve replied with his own smile. Both being good actors, it was a game they regularly played. "There's bound to be. It's well over a hundred years old, and I read in the guide over there on the desk that the Chalcot family have lived here since before the turn of the twentieth century. Apparently, they own or owned vast tracts of land, mostly given over to rubber and some fruit - might be pineapple, but I could be wrong."

"Really? Chalcot does ring a bell," Di replied, raising her eyebrows with interest.

"Well, I suppose it would. The last Chalcot was a life peer I believe, and the lady who now owns this place is an 'Honourable'."

"I told you! I bet they have some good stories to tell."

"Di! Haven't you had enough excitement recently? I would have thought two murders in our home village were too many for anyone. Apart from my business meeting tomorrow, we're here for a holiday. We both need a rest and Malaysia seemed far enough away for us to forget the dramas of Agios Mamas."

"Of course. Don't fuss so. I'm not looking for excitement, trouble or otherwise. I was just saying."

Steve gave her his 'old-fashioned' look which Di knew well. He didn't have to say any more. He could read her like a book.

"Come on then. Let's go downstairs. I'm dying for a cuppa."

~~~~~

The lounge held a commanding view overlooking a lawn which sloped towards a naturally wooded area. Through open doors, they could see flower beds bordering a pathway leading to a building situated some distance away. Squinting against the sun, Diana decided that in England, this building would have been declared a folly or at best a summer house.

Everywhere she looked, she was astounded at the vividness of the colours around her. Coming from Cyprus, they were used to a climate that was hot and dry. During the long summer months, plants mostly withered and died, leaving dusty dormant bushes and gasping wilting trees waiting for the life-giving winter rains. Here in Malaysia, a tropical monsoon climate created a fresh and colourful landscape. Huge hibiscus flowers in red, pink and yellow were arrayed with tall, stately lilies and flags. The trees were clothed in liana and hung with terracotta pots, each containing an orchid plant. Di was astonished at the variety in colour, shape and size of each flowering plant.

"Come and sit down, darling. The tea is here." Steve spoke from behind her.

Turning, Di walked back into the room, a delighted look upon her face.

"This place is just gorgeous. Have you seen all the orchids? I'd forgotten how beautiful the flowers are here. Did you know orchids represent the largest flower family in the plant kingdom?"

"No I didn't. How do you know that?" He passed a cup over to her.

Before she could answer, Di's attention was caught by a figure entering the lounge from the hallway. The woman's age was indeterminate and difficult to guess. She could have been anywhere between forty and late fifties. Small in height, she was almost skeletally thin and her mousey-coloured hair was cut short and straight. A pair of spectacles dangled around her neck, attached to a silver chain. She was dressed in a short-sleeved, white aertex shirt and slacks cut to mid-calf length. Catching sight of Diana and Steve, she paused and then as if changing her mind walked over to where they sat.

"Mr and Mrs Rivers, I believe. I'm Miss Chalcot, how do you do? Welcome to Kebun Pertama. I do hope you enjoy your stay here with us." Her voice was clipped and controlled. They would have expected nothing less from an 'Honourable'.

Steve immediately stood up to shake their hostess' hand, realising this was the owner of the hotel.

"How do you do?"

Diana took the outstretched hand in turn and wondered at the iciness of it. She found herself staring into a pair of grey, appraising eyes.

"Mrs Rivers, I've read your books."

"Oh." Diana felt a little nonplussed by Miss Chalcot's statement, not expecting it.

"Don't look so worried. I said 'books'. If I hadn't enjoyed the first, I certainly would not have bothered with the others."

"Thank you," Di mumbled.

"Yes, very entertaining. I can see why your style has been likened to a modern day Agatha Christie, although they contain a bit more sex I suppose. But you set a splendid scene and portray your characters well. You've invented some wonderful murders, and yet you do not dwell too much upon the blood and gore as some contemporary fiction does nowadays, thereby letting the readers use their own imagination. What are you working on at the moment, another mystery thriller for your series?"

For once, Diana was taken aback and found herself taking a breath. This woman's manner was so direct, almost intimidating.

"I-I've just finished a novel set in Cyprus and I haven't yet begun anything else," she stammered.

"Do you have a story in mind?"

"Um, nothing concrete, just a few ideas I've had playing around in my head for some time but nothing that's really grabbed my attention."

"Good. So you're doing nothing at the moment?" Again, Di felt like she was under interrogation and gave a slight shake of her head.

"Then you might be interested in looking through some old papers of mine."

"Oh. Well yes, yes of course." Di's heart sank. She had met so many people who thought they *'had a book in them'*. Ninety-nine times out of a hundred most of the stuff was unprintable.

Miss Chalcot obviously thought the matter was concluded, as she gave them a nod and left the lounge.

Sitting back down, Steve gave Di a wicked grin. "Well, that's curtailed you, my love."

"Yeah, nothing I like more than reading other people's masterpieces." She gave a sigh. "I could hardly have been rude and said 'no', could I?"

Chuckling at the sour look upon her face, Steve indicated their drinks. "Come on, finish your tea and we'll have a swim. The pool looks very inviting and there's a Jacuzzi somewhere here too. It will get rid of all your aches and pains from the flight."

"Sounds good to me. Spa baths also massage swollen legs, and I could do with a little help there. What time is your business appointment tomorrow?"

"Ten o'clock. Why? Do you want to come into KL with me?"

"No thanks. I think I'll just relax for a day or so. We've got over three glorious weeks - plenty of time to explore the city."

"Fine, I'll ask where the best shops are located, as I expect you'll want to replace half your wardrobe while we're here." He gave her a grin.

"Only half? Ha ha! Prices are bound to be reasonable and Cyprus is not the best place for clothes shopping. Yes, I'll be happy to spend a day or so looking."

This time, Steve gave a laugh. "You name me one woman who 'just looks'. I foresee my wallet being much lighter at the end of this holiday."

Chapter 2

Steve left for KL after breakfasting with Diana on their shady veranda. Despite the relative coolness of the morning, she could already feel the humidity rising.

Di tidied their room and slipped into her bathing costume. The longer than usual top covered her stomach and her bump was barely noticeable. After filling her beach bag with the necessities for a quiet swim followed by a read in the shade, Di left the room and walked down to the pool.

The clear, turquoise-coloured water looked enticing and she was soon doing some easy breaststroke laps of the pool.

Recognising the other guests from last night in the dining room, Di exchanged pleasantries while she swam. She had learned that their hotel was only half full, which accounted for the space and quietness about the place. Cool and refreshed, Di dried herself off and sat down with her e-reader for a morning of peaceful relaxation.

She had started a new novel on the flight but had only read two chapters. The story so far was far-fetched; the main character had begun to irritate her. She wondered if she was actually going to finish it. The writer had a good reputation, but Di felt she was trying too hard. There was just too much happening for the story to ring true. Di's mind wandered and putting the reader down, she examined her surroundings.

The hotel had begun life as a family home for the wealthy Chalcot family from England. The large house occupied a prominent position in the middle of the estate, and Di supposed the family money came from the rubber which was always in demand. Now the estate had diversified, like so many other businesses, with a hotel.

Beyond the pool, Di could see a building which resembled an English summer house. Built in brick and glass it was topped with a green-tiled roof which matched that of the main house. Despite its obvious English beginnings, the green tiles definitely gave an oriental feel to the place.

Restless with her tedious and unreadable book (she had now decided), Di thought she would go for a walk and explore more of the grounds. The day was heating up fast and she was glad she had remembered to bring her straw sunhat. She had suffered from sunstroke before, and Steve would be annoyed if she was careless again.

Following a gravel path meandering between neat flower-beds, she eventually arrived at the summer house. A shallow flight of steps led to a small patio with a large brick barbeque in one corner, and at the back of this paved area there was a pair of closed glass doors. Trying the door handle, she found they were unlocked. Inside, she saw a row of wooden table and chairs neatly stacked against a side wall, suggesting that the place was used as a function room for parties and private lunches.

"My father built this place on a whim. He really wanted a folly, but the local architect and builders couldn't or wouldn't understand what he was aiming for, so he ended up with this. We use it for wedding breakfasts or birthday parties, but mostly it's ignored. No air conditioning you see. I suppose I could get round to having it fitted, but it's hardly worth the bother."

Turning, Diana met those grey, appraising eyes again. She was standing just inside the doorway and Di couldn't understand how she had failed to hear her footsteps on the gravel outside.

"I think it's lovely. I've always fancied a place like this, but we haven't the room and like you, I doubt we'd use it enough to justify the expense."

"Oh, Father didn't worry about expense. If he wanted something, he just took or bought it."

Di couldn't help recognising the touch of bitterness in Miss Chalcot's voice. She felt a frisson of excitement well up within her. She just knew there was some mystery concerning this family and place. "About those papers you mentioned yesterday, would you like me to take a look sometime?"

"Yes please. When would be convenient? I realise this is a holiday for you but--"

Much more interested than twenty-four hours ago, Di interrupted her, "How about now?"

~~~~~

Diana was surprised on entering Miss Chalcot's private study; the room was out of keeping with the rest of the light and airy house. It was dark and sombre, more masculine than feminine. Old English hunting prints adorned the walls, together with a collection of photographs which Di supposed were family portraits. An enormous desk took up almost the entire right-hand wall with a huge chair behind it. Set into another wall were French windows which led to a partitioned balcony. Because of the sloping lawn, this part of the building was higher than the rest and the balcony was set some feet from the ground, not high enough to deter determined intruders, but enough to give a lofty view of the grounds.

Casting an eye round the study, she noticed a photograph of a beautiful blonde woman in her wedding gown, while another portrayed a tall brunette with striking good looks. Amongst these, there were various poses of children at different stages in their lives. Di couldn't discern how many there were or to whom they belonged and she didn't know her hostess well enough to comment or ask.

Ignoring Diana's obvious interest in her family portraits, Miss Chalcot indicated Diana should join her at her desk. "Here you'll find some interesting reading no doubt," she said, casting a hand over a pile of slim, leather-bound volumes lying on the polished wood.

Diana turned from the photographs and walked over to join her. Picking a book up at random, she flicked open the pages exclaiming, "Why, it's a diary!"

"They all are," Miss Chalcot agreed drily.

Diana looked up at her words. "So what exactly would you like me to do with them?" she asked. She turned over another page, noting the small, neat handwriting. "Are they yours?"

"Um no, not really, mostly they're my mother's. I would like you to write them into a book. It doesn't have to be a biography. In fact, I'd prefer it to be written as a novel. Can you do that?"

"Ye-es. It depends on the content and whether it catches my interest."

"Oh, you'll find it interesting enough. There's plenty to get your teeth into."

"But why? Forgive me, but why me? Why don't you do it yourself?"

There was a pause. Miss Chalcot looked away, and Diana noticed a spasm cross her face before she replied.

"Because I don't have time. When I recognised your name on the booking form, I took it as a sign. I knew you for an acclaimed author of repute and considered you the best person for recording our story."

"I appreciate that. I am flattered you consider me worthy. But this is about you. I think if you write it, with your family name and everything, it will sell better."

"I'm neither interested in selling nor marketing it, and I've just told you I haven't the time."

"I understand, time is precious and I'm busy too..." Di's voice trailed away as she caught the stricken look on Miss Chalcot's face.

"You don't understand." Again there was a pause. "I'll pay you handsomely. I just don't have time, full stop. Perhaps not even a month."

Shaken, Diana felt a shock pass through her as she realised what she was saying.

"I have untreatable pancreatic cancer, and the doctors and surgeons have done all they can. This is important to me. I have this yearning for the complete family history to be recorded accurately and put in order. It should have been done years ago. I should have done it, but I let the years slip by and want to put things straight while there is still time."

Diana didn't know what to say. She was embarrassed by her earlier reticence to help the woman. "I'm very sorry. That's such awful bad luck. An uncle of mine had the same and he lived for four years after the treatment, maybe you--"

"Maybe. But for now they've told me to expect the worst. I was stupid and delayed seeking medical help when I had the first symptoms. Now I'm to pay for my stupidity. It is nobody's fault but my own, and I'm prepared for my death, but first I have to put one or two things straight."

Realising Miss Chalcot had made up her mind; Diana knew she would take no advice from a stranger. Diana recognised her as being strong-willed, stubborn and used to having her own way.

"Okay. So if I take this project on, am I to understand that you want me to make a story from your family's history?"

"No, I want you to take it from my mother's entry into the Chalcot family when she married my father up to the final diary entry. You'll soon get the gist."

"May I ask? Are there any other members of your family still living?"

Again, there was a brief pause. "I have a sister. She lives in England."

"I see." Diana did. From Miss Chalcot's terse reply, Diana guessed there was some bad feeling between them, and as she obviously wasn't going to say anything else at that time, Diana had to ignore it.

"Well, I'd better make a start. I'll read through the diaries and give it some thought."

"We haven't discussed your fee yet."

It was Diana's turn to pause while she thought. "Let me have a read-through first. If I like the idea and consider I have the makings of a creditable novel, then we'll talk about it."

Diana felt *she* had to keep control of the situation. Miss Chalcot was educated and strong-minded. It would be all too easy for her to completely dictate terms on her home turf. Diana was her own woman and would not let herself be bullied. She didn't need the work, but she was interested enough to read about this mysterious woman and her life. She had a sudden premonition that these diaries were likely to wake some sleeping dragons.........................

"Children of the Plantation" is now available as an eBook and Paperback

Find out more about **Faith Mortimer** and her books at:
www.faithmortimerauthor.com
www.facebook.com/FaithMortimer.Author
http://twitter.com/FaithMortimer

Thank you!

Lightning Source UK Ltd.
Milton Keynes UK
UKOW031334170112

185555UK00011B/52/P